Five wa...
your lif...

1.   ...l help ... the e...
     e...-c...   li...

mark in the cut-throat world of The Music Industry.

3. Hopefully my boyish charm and ability to pull older girls will rub off on you and your love life will improve by 150% (and yes, I know that's not a real percentage, but go with it).

4. It will give you the confidence to try new things—marvel at my sophisticated taste in international cuisine and, um, wine gums . . .

5. You won't fail to impress your friends if you take note of my excellent people management skills. When it comes to dealing with hotshot executives, burly security men, and my mates, I think you'll find I am practically an expert.

So go ahead, read on and let me inspire... why are you laughing? That's so not cool . . .)

Here's a taste of what's to come . . .

'Hey!' Jackson snapped his fingers at me. 'Dum-dum! What are you staring at?'

'I have a suggestion,' I said.

He looked at me sceptically, but pointed at a chair anyway. I guess he must have been desperate.

I sat down and double-checked with the control room that this was really what I wanted to do.

'You say you haven't got a support act for the Marcy Slick tour,' I said. 'I say, if you walk down the corridor and enter recording studio two, you will find one.'

Jackson stared at me open-mouthed. Then he laughed. Hard. He even banged the table with his fist.

'You think your boys should be the opening act for Marcy Slick?' he roared. 'Are you TRIPPING?'

'I promise you they're ready,' I said.

'Ready?' he cried. 'The only thing those clowns are ready for is the Job Centre. Yesterday I went down there and the stupid one was FaceTiming with a crab!'

'It's actually a lobster,' I said. 'But that's beside the point. Look, they can do it. Don't forget—performing live was how they got their reputation in the first place. They will smash it.'

Jackson frowned. 'You really think so?'

I nodded. 'That's what's wrong with them. They're hungry for the roar of the crowd. Once you get them out there with the people, the album will follow straight away.'

He sighed. 'I don't know—it's a hell of a risk.'

'It isn't,' I said. 'But if it all goes wrong, I will take full responsibility. I will go with them on the road and help keep them in line.'

Jackson sat back in his chair and stared at the ceiling.

'They would be a lot cheaper than the Clean League.'

'The cheapest,' I said. 'Just give them a chance.'

He sat forward again and stared at me. His eyes were so piercing, they almost took my attention away from his daft hair.

'Fine,' he said. 'But this goes wrong and it's your ass, not mine.'

For the baby formerly known as Larry.

OXFORD
UNIVERSITY PRESS

Great Clarendon Street, Oxford OX2 6DP
Oxford University Press is a department of the University of Oxford.
It furthers the University's objective of excellence in research, scholarship,
and education by publishing worldwide in

Oxford New York

Oxford is a registered trademark of Oxford University Press
in the UK and in certain other countries

Text Copyright © Ben Davis 2017
Illustrations Copyright © Mike Lowery 2017

The moral rights of the author and illustrator have been asserted

Database right Oxford University Press (maker)

First published 2017

British Library Cataloguing in Publication Data

Data available

ISBN: 978-0-19-274795-2

1 3 5 7 9 10 8 6 4 2

Printed in Great Britain
Paper used in the production of this book is a natural,
recyclable product made from wood grown in sustainable forests.
The manufacturing process conforms to the environmental
regulations of the country of origin.

All photographic images from Shutterstock and OUP

THE PRIVATE BLOG OF

JOE COWLEY

WRITTEN BY
BEN DAVIS

STRAIGHT OUTTA
NERDSVILLE

HIGH LIFE HIGHLAND	
3800 17 0030465 6	
Askews & Holts	Nov-2017
JF	£6.99

OXFORD
UNIVERSITY PRESS

Oh, blog.

BLOG!

You have NO IDEA how happy I am right now. I'm smiling so much, I look like the Joker in a wind tunnel.

GET A LOAD OF THIS.

• Since the beginning of the year, Harry, Ad, Greeny, and me have been living in our own flat, right in the middle of London. Amazing, or what? We're living the dream in the Big Smoke, independent for the first time in our lives. I mean, yes, we do have to live with Mrs Gleba, our chaperone, and yes, she is incredibly strict, and yes, we do have an eleven o'clock curfew, and yes, she did once whack me with a spatula for mild blasphemy, but the point is, the small-town rubes we once were are dead and gone. We are now city-slickin', hard-hustlin', tube-ridin', good-timin', not-even-missin'-our-mummies-one-little-bit London boys.

• It's all because the ꙅOUND EXPERIENCE (Harry, Ad, and Greeny's electro-techno-dubstep-whatever-the-hell-they-are group) has been signed up by PGS Records. They've already recorded a demo with MC Camelface, but soon we will be launching their career—signing their first record contract with the executive who is going to be in charge of their careers.

- What's even better is I am their manager. Me. Joe Cowley, with my four Bs, three Cs, and two Ds at GCSE, a big-time music manager. Well, not manager, exactly. The term the record company is using is 'intern'. But it sounds proper important, doesn't it?

- The other week, I got rid of my braces. Finally, my teeth are free of the mouth cage of doom!

- You'd think that would be enough, but it isn't. Check this out, blog. I have a girlfriend! And I am proper mad about her.

Of course, this is just between you and me. I would never tell the guys. It would totally ruin the cool, bachelor vibe we've got going on, but I really am. Mila is so amazing. Since we met at *BUZZFEST*, and she punched Mr Boocock in the face when he was trying to beat me up at my mum's wedding (long story), we've been inseparable, Skyping every night when I was still in Tammerstone and exploring London together. We've done all the touristy stuff—held hands on Tower Bridge, gazed at each other lovingly on the London Eye and tongue-kissed in the Tate Modern.

« Older posts

I mean, yes, Mrs Gleba has a strict NO GIRLS ALLOWED rule, and Mila's dad is back living with them, along with her two sisters, so we can't exactly have any 'alone time', but that will work itself out, I know it.

All the rough times are in the past. I've left Tammerstone and all the other losers behind, and now I can reinvent myself. I mean, check this out: remember that control room in my head that used to help me make decisions and basically wreck my life? It has completely disappeared. Gone forever. And do you know why? Because I don't need it any more. That's right, blog. It's goodbye, nerd Joe, and hello, sophisticated man-about-town Joseph.

The world is my oyster. It's time to show it who's boss.

Tuesday 4th February

Had a bit of a mishap today.

I was walking through Covent Garden after lunch with Mila. She had gone off to meet some friends, and I was heading back to the flat. It had stopped raining and the air was nice and crisp. I must have been too busy enjoying the sights, because the next thing I knew, I had bumped into this bloke. I apologized and went to move on but he called me back.

'You bloody idiot,' he cried. 'You broke my glasses!'

He picked them up off the floor. Sure enough, the lens had fallen out. Ah crap.

'I am so sorry,' I said. 'I didn't see you.'

The man puffed his cheeks out. His face was all red and he smelled like dusty farts. 'I can't afford to get these fixed. What am I supposed to do?'

I swallowed hard. This was a bad situation. I had to try to put it right. 'How much would it cost to repair them?'

He held the glasses up to the light. 'Forty quid.'

I pulled out my wallet. 'I've only got thirty.'

He leaned over and snatched the notes out of my hand. 'That'll do.'

I walked away, relieved. It shows how streetwise I am now. Tammerstone me would have handled that horribly.

9.30 p.m.

Thought the flat could do with some sophisticated furniture like bookshelves and stuff, so headed out to the *IKEA* in Wembley. The others wouldn't come with me because they were halfway through a *Game of Thrones* marathon. Idiots.

Anyway, *IKEA* is kind of like *Game of Thrones* if you think about it. It's confusing, there are loads of weird names, and everyone looks like they're about to do a murder.

Sadly, I soon realized that there was no way I'd get a flat-pack on the Tube, so all I ended up with was a bellyful of meatballs, a couple of candle holders, and as many tiny pencils as my pockets could hold.

« Older posts

Thursday 6th February

Last night, me and Mila went to see this new experimen-
tal play called Isolation. I'd explain what it was about, but
I have no cocking clue. It was just a bloke in a leotard
flapping around on stage pretending to be a duck. Crap.
Plus, they didn't sell little tubs of ice cream in the interval.
I mean, what kind of crummy theatre was this?

When we got outside, Mila kept going on about how
'thought-provoking' it was, and I didn't want to seem like a
dumbo, so I agreed with her. I overheard this bloke in the
toilets going on about how it was reminiscent of Marx so I
repeated that.

Mila gasped and said, 'Wow, you're so insightful.'

Thank you, toilet man. To be honest, I don't even know
what Marx's first name is. For all I know, it could be Skid.

'You know, Joe,' Mila said to me, swinging my hand as
we walked. 'I'm meeting a friend on Tottenham Court Road
first thing tomorrow morning.'

'Um, OK.'

'And that's really close to your flat, isn't it?'

'I suppose it is.' My knowledge of London is a little shaky.
Turns out it's way more complicated than Monopoly boards
would have you believe.

'Well,' she went on, 'don't you think it would be easier if I
stayed over with you?'

Blood rushed to my face, neck, and various other

locations. I mean, stay over? What did that mean?

'B-but Mrs Gleba says you're not allowed in,' I said.

Mila stopped, pulled me close and kissed me. 'Listen, Joe. Mrs Gleba can't stay awake all night, can she?'

I gulped. 'No?'

'Well then let's go,' she said, as Big Ben donged for the tenth time.

My heart pounded like mad all the way home. I don't know why. I was probably just going to sleep on the floor and let her have my bed. The only reason she was staying was convenience.

When we got in, everyone had gone to bed. Phew.

We tiptoed across the open-plan living room/kitchen and into the corridor where the bedrooms are. Luckily, mine is the first one you come to, so we didn't have to cross Mrs Gleba's doorway.

I grabbed my knob and twisted it.

Hold on, you do know that by knob, I mean doorknob, right? I've just realized that last bit sounds pervy. And painful.

As I was saying, I was about to enter my room, when a creaking door and a toilet flush cut through the silence.

Oh no! Not Mrs Gleba!

I breathed a sigh of relief when I saw the figure silhouetted in the bathroom light. It was just Ad. He stopped dead in the doorway and cocked his head.

« Older posts

'Is someone there?' he yelled.

'Yes, Ad,' I whispered. 'It's Joe. Now please, be quiet.'

Ad squinted into the darkness. He wasn't wearing his glasses, which meant he was basically blind. 'How do I know it's really you and not some burglar?'

Mila giggled behind me.

'Um, because a burglar wouldn't have my exact voice,' I said.

Ad rubbed his chin. 'You might just be a burglar that's proper good at impressions, though. I'm going ask you a question only Joe would know the answer to.'

I thought about just going into my room with Mila and closing the door, but Ad would probably follow me. One thing I've learned about him these past few weeks is that he doesn't have the same boundaries as other people.

'All right, I've thought of one,' he said. 'Who is Joe's favourite **STAR TREK** captain?'

I sighed. 'Captain Picard.'

'Wrong,' said Ad. 'Kirk.'

I couldn't take any more of this. Ad is always getting Kirk and Picard confused and he knows how angry that makes me. I turned on the light.

'There,' I said. 'It's me. Can I go now?'

Ad squinted at us. 'Oh yeah, all right, Joe. Hey, Mila!' he yelled. 'How's it going?'

Before she could say anything, Mrs Gleba's bedroom door flew open and she stomped out. As scary as she looks in the day, night-time Mrs Gleba is something else altogether—like a rhino with curlers in.

'So, you think you can pull the wool over Mrs Gleba's eyes, eh?' she barked. 'No girls.'

'But, Mrs Gleba,' I protested, 'she's not my girlfriend. She's my . . . tutor. She's tuting me.'

Mrs Gleba shook her head and grabbed Mila's arm. 'The only thing she teaches you is how to be idiot. And you already big idiot.'

Mila yelped in pain as Mrs Gleba squeezed, but before she knew it, she was out the door.

On her way back to her room, Mrs Gleba pointed a saveloy finger at me and said, 'I catch you disobeying me again, there'll be big trouble, you understand?'

I nodded, wallowing in the horrible knowledge that I won't be eighteen, and thus, chaperone-free, for over a year.

I went to Ad's room to have a go at him for dropping me in it, but when I got in there he was doing naked press-ups and a little bit of me wished I was blind.

Friday 7th February

We decided that because the hard work of elevating the 𝑆𝑂𝑈𝑁𝐷 𝐸𝑋𝑃𝐸𝑅𝐼𝐸𝑁𝐶𝐸 to global superstardom was about to start, we should have one last weekend of carefree city fun. Last Saturday, we played Epic Warfare and built blanket forts, but I decided that we have outgrown such childish things now. Tonight, we are playing poker.

I headed into town to buy a deck of cards and some

smokes. The cards weren't a problem, but the cigar shop was another thing entirely.

'Give me a box of your finest Cubans, squire,' I said to the bloke behind the counter.

That's how I talk now, blog. I am super mature. Then again, I've always had a wisdom beyond my years. I remember this one time when my Science teacher said 'penis' and I didn't even giggle. And it was a really odd thing to come out with at a parents' evening.

The cigar guy looked up at me over his copy of the *Sun*. 'How old are you?'

'Eighteen,' I replied, making my voice all deep and manly just to be sure.

He pulled a face like he didn't really believe me but couldn't be arsed asking for ID. 'A box of our best Cubans costs five hundred pounds.'

FIVE HUNDRED? Time for a rethink.

'OK, how about a box of your cheapest Cubans?'

'A hundred.'

I gulped. Why the hell are cigars so expensive? They are basically tubby cigarettes.

'OK,' I said, still trying to maintain my cool dude stance. 'I'm going to level with you, my friend. I need a box of your cheapest cigars.'

The bloke grunted and fetched me a box of Sutkuses— four for a tenner. Now, that's more like it.

« Older posts

'So where are these from?' I asked as he rang up my purchase. 'Somewhere near Cuba?'

The bloke chuckled. 'If you consider Lithuania near Cuba.'

I scurried home with my cards and box of fine Lithuanians. Mum texted, as she does every day, to check that I'm OK and that I haven't been people-trafficked. I fired off a quick reply as I cut through the bustle of Covent Garden. Yes, everything's fine, stop worrying, blah, blah, blah.

I was about to hit send when I heard a yell a little bit ahead. Someone else had walked into that bloke and broke his glasses again. And after I had just paid to have them repaired!

It was then that a realization dawned on me—something only city-boy Joseph would figure out: that bloke needs to be more careful with his eyewear.

Back at the flat, I shuffled the cards (this took ages because I don't know how to do it properly) and set the table. We had bowls of snacks and cold (non-alcoholic) beers ready to go.

'Right, gentlemen,' I said. 'What's say we light up?'

The others nodded so I lit the cigars on the gas hob. While I did that, Harry put some music on.

'It's a Buzz Algonquin playlist, old beans,' he explained. 'So we're prepared.'

Buzz Algonquin is producing the *SOUND EXPERIENCE*'s first album. Harry and Ad chose him because he is experimental. When they told me this, I just nodded and smiled as if I had any idea who the cocking hell he is.

'These cigars, old son,' said Harry, uncertainly sniffing his. 'They have an . . . unusual aroma.'

'Unusual's right,' said Greeny. 'They smell like sewage.'

'*Burnt* sewage,' said Ad, wrinkling his nose.

'Now now,' I said. '**Men's Domain** says that cigars are a "required taste" and that we shouldn't let their "bouquet" put us off.'

I tried to control my gag reflex as I took a puff. Nothing really happened. I tried again. All it left me with was little bits of brown grit on the end of my tongue.

'How is it, Joe?' said Ad.

I took the cigar out of my mouth and examined it as if it were some kind of antique. 'She's a difficult smoke, but I have a feeling she's worth it,' I said. I know people refer to boats as 'she' so I guess the same applies to cigars.

Harry took a puff. Nothing seemed to happen for him, either. It was weird seeing him smoking anything other than his empty pipe. He looked at the end as if there was something wrong with it.

Ad took a drag. Greeny sighed and said something about how he misses Scott, his boyfriend back home in Tammerstone (WE KNOW, YOU TELL US EVERY FIVE

« Older posts

SECONDS), before having a puff.

'Right,' I said. 'Now we're all lit up, let's play. I'll deal this round.'

I put the cigar in my mouth and dealt us each five cards. We all picked them up and examined them closely, quietly contemplating our first moves.

'Lads,' said Ad, breaking the quiet. 'Do any of you know how to play poker?'

Another hush descended as we all glanced at each other.

'I don't,' said Greeny. 'Do you, Harry?'

Harry frowned as he stared at his cards. 'Not a bloody clue, old bean. I'm sure Joe must.'

They all stared at me. 'Um, well, you see . . .'

'Great,' said Harry. 'So we've organized a poker night and none of us know how to play?'

I couldn't believe it. When you see guys playing poker in films, they just sit down and do it. They don't have to learn. I thought it was just one of those things that comes with being a man of the world, like knowing how to change a tyre or understanding what the stock market is.

Before I could answer, Mrs Gleba's bedroom door opened and she stomped in like an angry woolly mammoth.

'Ooh,' she groaned with her hands over her nose and mouth. 'So that's what that smell is. I thought one of you had gone ah-ah in your pants.'

She walked around the table plucking the cigars out of our mouths. 'There is no smoking in here. You know the rules.'

Yes, of course, how could I forget the rules?

1. No smoking.
2. No drinking.
3. NO GIRLS!

None of the others complained. I think they were relieved they didn't have to smell them any more.

Mrs Gleba was about to run all the cigars under the tap when she stopped and started laughing. 'You idiot boys— to smoke cigars you have to cut off the end. You must have been sucking until you were blue in the faces!'

Ah, so that explains it. I made a mental note for next time. When we go in to sign the contracts on Monday, they'll probably have actual Cubans, so I don't want us to look stupid.

Mrs Gleba disposed of the stinky Lithuanian cigars and trundled over to the table. 'What are you boys playing?'

'Poker,' I replied, still trying to seem cool and Bond-like even though I'm pretty sure 007 never had his smokes confiscated by his chaperone.

'No playing for money,' she barked. 'My rat-bastard ex-husband lost our car to gambling. If you play for something, you play for my solozhenick.'

Solozhenick is a Ukrainian pudding. It's basically a jam roly-poly but rank.

Once she'd gone back to bed, we decided we might as well make the best of a bad time and play cards. The only problem was, the only game we all know how to play is Snap.

Still, it was the most sophisticated game of Snap that has ever been played.

Saturday 8th February

I felt a bit deflated after our attempt at a classy gentlemen's evening went south last night. I'm not going to go into too much detail, but let's just say it ended with Harry and Ad ordering a pizza for a Mr Hugh G. Rection.

Anyway, I was heading out to buy some milk from the offy, when something made me stop and listen. I was standing on the stairs and could hear a voice in the lobby.

'Yeah, everyone's going to be there,' the voice said. 'Plus, there's going to be cocktails, wine, fondue. Yes, fondue.'

I crept down so I could get a better look. It was one of the women that lives in the penthouse.

'Be here any time. Gerhart and Ole are coming about eight.'

Gerhart? Ole? Fondue? Sounded like my kind of party. But there was just the small matter of getting invited. I decided to head back to the flat and confer with the others.

'This would be a first for us, wouldn't it, old beans?' said

Harry. 'A penthouse party.'

'It'd be wicked,' said Ad. 'We might find out some American army secrets.'

'What are you on about, old son?' said Harry.

'You know?' said Ad. 'The American army place—the Penthouse.'

'The Pentagon, Ad—the Pentagon,' I said after an awkward silence. 'Anyway, we're going to go, right? I mean, this is a golden opportunity.'

'Too bloody right, soldier. It's not every day one gets to soiree with ravishing penthouse ladies,' said Harry. 'I've run into them once or twice, and I'm sure I caught one of them giving me a lingering look over the recycling.'

'Um, you have a girlfriend, don't you?' said Greeny.

Harry chuckled and puffed on his empty pipe. 'Affirmative. But there's no harm in an innocent flirt, is there?'

'Plus, they're travelling around Europe,' said Ad. 'It don't count if you're in a different country.'

It's true—not the different country thing, that's ridiculous, but the travelling thing. Harry's and Ad's girlfriends are spending six months exploring Europe. You should see their Instagram—it's infuriating.

'So how does this work?' Greeny asked. 'We can't just crash their party, can we?'

We sat around the table and contemplated how we were going to do it. The last time we tried anything like this, it was Year Ten and we got caught trying to sneak into Ellie Baker's party dressed as pizza delivery men. It was Harry's fake Italian accent that rumbled us.

'I've got it, old beans,' Harry said, slapping the table.

'I think I have as well,' said Ad.

Harry raised an eyebrow at me. 'Let's hear yours first, then.'

Ad leaned forward and lowered his voice. 'One word,' he said. 'Knock and run.'

Harry, Greeny, and me looked at each other as if to decide who was going to take this one.

'OK, old boy,' said Harry, biting the bullet. 'So guide us through it, then. First, we knock?'

Ad nodded.

'Then we run?'

Ad nodded again.

'Then what?'

Ad raised a finger, then retracted it. Then he frowned at the table for a bit.

'Good effort, old boy,' said Harry, patting Ad's shoulder. 'So here's my suggestion—we're their neighbours, correct?'

I nodded.

'And is it not customary for neighbours to bring each other gifts?'

I narrowed my eyes. 'What are you saying?'

« Older posts

'I'm saying we go and pay them a neighbourly visit with a bottle of something, and . . . "Oh what's this? You're having a party? Well, it would be rude not to join you for a quick beverage."'

He leaned back and took a satisfied puff of his pipe.

'That might actually work,' I said.

'Except for one thing,' Greeny cut in. 'How do we bring a bottle when we haven't got any?'

'We have,' said Ad, getting up and opening a cupboard. 'Here we go—vinegar, ketchup.'

'I'll take care of it,' I said. 'Mila's nineteen—maybe I can get her to bring one.'

Before anyone could say anything else, Mrs Gleba's door flew open and she stuck her head out.

'What are you talking about?' she said. 'I heard you mention hussy mama's name.'

'Oh no, I didn't say her name,' I said. 'I actually said . . . "meal out", as in, tonight we're having a "meal out".'

Mrs Gleba eyeballed all of us individually then said, 'Remember, eleven o'clock curfew,' before stomping back into her room.

1 a.m.

'Right,' I said to the lads on the landing outside the penthouse. 'I've consulted Men's Domain and found some tips for us.'

Harry chuckled. 'You and that bloody website. Why can't you just go in and be yourself?'

'Are you mental?' said Greeny. 'You've seen what happens when he does that, yeah?'

'Good point, old bean,' said Harry. 'I suppose we should hear these tips, then.'

1. Prepare some amusing anecdotes.

'Ah, we've got loads of those, old bean,' said Harry. 'What's say we regale them with the story of the time we threw piss balloons at Gav James?'

2. Bring a gift.

'Done,' said Ad, holding up a bottle we found at the back of a cupboard. We had no idea what it was because the label was in Ukrainian, but it definitely counted as a gift. The whole Mila bringing one plan didn't work out because she's got to go out with her family and won't be over until later.

3. Dress sharp.

I'd taken care of that one and ensured that we were coordinated, with matching black suits and ties. I reckoned we looked proper professional. Greeny agreed, then ruined it by saying, 'Under-takers are professionals, right?'

I knocked on the door and the woman I saw in the lobby answered. She frowned and said, 'Can I help you?'

'Um, we're from number fifty-three,' I said. 'And we just thought we'd bring you this bottle as a token of our esteem.'

She looked at the bottle with a raised eyebrow. 'Koloch . . . nach . . . tikov. Sounds exotic.'

'It is,' said Harry. 'It's from Ukraine. Our . . . friend from there recommended it.'

'How international of you,' she said, with a little smile.

'That ain't the half of it,' said Ad. 'Joe's girlfriend is Holland-ish.'

Note to self: next time we go to a sophisticated party, gag Ad.

'Well, as you've brought us a bottle I suppose I should invite you in,' she said.

SUCCESS!

She led us inside, while Harry mouthed something at me about how she was the one who totally fancied him.

The penthouse was amazing. Our flat's pretty swanky,

but this place made it look like Mad Morris's bus shelter. Everyone there looked dead smart. They were all older than us, but not ridiculously old like my mum or something. I could already tell this was the kind of grown-up London party we should have been attending all along.

'My name's Tabitha,' she said. 'Would you boys like some canapés?'

'No ta,' said Ad. 'I promised my mum I'd stay away from drugs.'

Luckily, Tabitha laughed, then said, 'Right, let's see that Ukrainian stuff.'

I handed it over.

Another woman appeared from the kitchen, holding a tray of yet more canapés. There were no cheese and pineapples on sticks, which my old non-sophisticated Tammerstone self would have been outraged about.

'This is my flatmate, Maddie,' said Tabitha. 'Maddie, these are the boys from fifty-three.'

I waved. I mean, what the hell? Who waves at a party? I turned the wave into a nose scratch sharpish and said hi instead.

'You lads are over eighteen, aren't you?' Maddie asked.

« Older posts

We looked at each other. No one was saying anything. I guessed it was going to be up to me. 'Y-yeah, of course we are,' I said. 'How do you think we bought this . . . drink?'

God, I hoped it wasn't drain unblocker.

'Wicked,' said Maddie, who is quite possibly the poshest person I've ever met. 'Then you'll join us in a wee snifter?'

Ad spluttered with laughter. 'Huh huh huh, wee snifter.'

I subtly trod on his foot before turning back to Maddie. 'Sounds great!'

'Oh, none for me, thanks,' said Greeny. 'I'm straight edge.'

Harry nodded. 'Yes, me too.'

'That goes for me and all,' said Ad. 'I'm straight ledge.'

'Looks like it's just the three of us, then,' said Tabitha, filling three tiny glasses with the clear liquid. 'Bottoms up!'

I ignored Ad giggling again, picked up one of the glasses and sniffed it. Oh my God, I think it may have singed my nose hairs.

'On the count of three,' said Maddie. 'One, two . . .'

Maddie and Tabitha lifted their glasses and knocked their drinks back in one go. At the same time, I lifted mine, but wussed out at the last second and threw it over my shoulder into a potted plant.

When I looked up, Maddie and Tabitha were wiping tears from their eyes. 'Wow, that stuff has a kick,' said Tabitha.

'I think my insides are burning,' said Maddie, looking at

me. 'Hey, what's your name?'

'Um, Joe,' I said, hoping they hadn't noticed their plant withering.

'Joe is hard core,' she said. 'Look, he hasn't been affected by it.'

'Incredible,' said Harry. 'It's almost as if he didn't drink it at all!'

After that, the party went like a dream. I accidentally (not) let slip that the boys are in a band that is attached to *PGS Records* and Tabitha and Maddie got super excited and took us around the room, introducing us to their friends.

And what friends—never before have I encountered such luminaries. There were artists, writers, gallery owners. At my family parties, the closest thing we have to an artist is my cousin Dibble, who Sharpies willies on toilet cubicles.

Plus, I finally discovered the secret of surviving social events—don't talk. All I did was listen and occasionally chip in with a 'fascinating' or 'intriguing'.

It was even better when Mila arrived because she's pretty posh, so she fit right in. I looked around and the other guys seemed to be enjoying it, too. Even Ad. I overheard one bloke say he wanted to write a freeform jazz odyssey about him. He'd call it 'Space Cadet'.

It was all going so well that we lost track of time. Mila and me had been chatting to another couple for over an hour. They were both artisanal bakers who made political egg custards and we were about to arrange to meet up and sample some. It felt good to finally have grown-up conversations with real London people. I mean, our flat is great and everything, but the talk isn't exactly intellectual. The other day, we nearly got into a fight over whether you should sit down or stand up to wipe your bum (IT'S SIT DOWN AND ANYONE WHO TELLS YOU OTHERWISE IS A MONSTER).

Anyway, Claude was looking for a business card to give us when the door flew open. Everyone turned and stared. In such a civilized environment, the bang was shocking.

'What time are you calling this?' Mrs Gleba yelled.

Oh. Crap. I glanced at my watch. It was midnight.

'Do you think I am giving you boys curfew for the good of my health?' she boomed. 'Get to your rooms, now!'

Tabitha carefully approached Mrs Gleba. 'Can I help you, madam?'

'Don't madam me, hussy mama. You invite children to party?'

Claude and Marie stared at me as if I were a leper. I mean, how did they know it was me Mrs Gleba was talking about? It could just as easily have been Gabriel, the experimental bongo poet.

'I'm sorry,' said Tabitha, 'but they told us they were eighteen.'

Mrs Gleba glared at all four of us. 'Then they dirty stinky liars. If I was their mother I am putting them over my knee.'

Oh God, this was the worst thing ever. I could feel all my grown-up sophisticated credibility running away from me like so much Camembert fondue.

'Wait, what is this?' Mrs Gleba stomped into the flat and picked up the bottle of Kalachlachlachlachlach. 'Not only are they dirty rule breakers and dirty liars but they also dirty thief? That's it!'

She reached across the table, grabbed Harry and Ad by their ears and dragged them out of the flat. Then she came back and did the same to Greeny.

I looked for an escape but found none. No matter where I hid, I knew Mrs Gleba would find me. She has a nose like a bloodhound. She also has a really good sense of smell.

Before I knew it, I felt the cold fingers of doom clamp around my ear and I was ferociously dragged out of the party. Other than the squeak of my freshly polished shoes on the wooden floor, the whole room was silent.

'Um, Claude, Marie,' I said. 'We'll meet up some time in the week, yeah?'

They wouldn't make eye contact.

'No good for you?' I said. 'OK, how about next weekend? Sunday is best for me.'

Nothing.

'Um, I'll see you soon, Mila,' I said.

Mila winced. 'Yeah, bye, Joe.'

Ugh, I can't believe it. I had it right there in my hands. I was going to be an urbane Londonite with friends with names like Jocasta and Peregrine. Mila was going to finally think I was cool enough for her and not some hillbilly from the sticks. It was going to be a new Joe—a rebirth. Then it was all snatched from me by a demon in an apron.

Sunday 9th February

Today has got even worse. Got up this morning to find that Mrs Gleba has hidden the Xbox and Sky remote as punishment.

'Honestly, Mrs Gleba,' I said, while she made us a 'penance breakfast' of muesli and dry brown toast. 'We didn't intend any disrespect, we just lost track of time.'

She waved me off. 'You are thinking Mrs Gleba is being born yesterday. I heard the same excuse from my rat-bastard ex-husband. "I lose track of time, I only have two drink, I trip and land in Anichka the milk maid's bed." I don't want to hear more. Now, sit. Eat toast. You too skinny.'

God, it's depressing. Mrs Gleba is completely cramping our style. How can we become refined city slickers with her around?

Still, as soon as we sign our contracts tomorrow, I'm sure we'll get invited to loads of swanky record company parties where everyone is cool and there are bouncers on the door to keep out insane, ear-twisting chaperones.

Monday 10th February

The big day. The *SOUND EXPERIENCE* were being signed by *PGS Records* for a two-album deal and I'm going to work for them.

It is huge. Massive. Humassive. That's the only word I can think of to describe it.

I got the other guys up super early. Greeny kept whinging that he didn't even need to be there because he just did visual effects, but I told him that we are a band of brothers,

« Older posts

all for one and one for all. Plus, Greeny is a big part of the band's appeal—gay, nerdy, now ridiculously athletic. He had to be there. Scott would have to wait for his daily three-hour phone call.

I made sure we left the flat at nine, even though the meeting wasn't scheduled until twelve. This meant that we were sitting in the waiting room at PGS ninety minutes early.

It's a proper impressive place—a swish skyscraper overlooking the Thames. Inside, everything is black and white—even the pictures of their most successful artists. Just looking at them sent a shiver down my spine. Soon, the *SOUND EXPERIENCE* will join them. Maybe they'll become legends.

When the time came, we were ushered into an office down the corridor by a sharp-suited secretary. There was a huge fish tank taking up an entire wall. I suppose when you see it you're supposed to be impressed, but I was mainly wondering who has to clean it out. I used to have a couple of goldfish and they did massive poos. Imagine the horror that would come out of a shark's arse.

The bloke sitting behind the desk didn't look like your typical record company type. He was about forty-ish, wearing jeans and a *Chronic Tremor* T-shirt. He was on the phone, but smiled and winked at us as we sat down.

'Yeah, you tell him the *Buzzards* won't get out of bed for less than fifty K!' he said.

My gaze drifted to the top of his head. There was something weird about his hair. I couldn't quite figure out what.

'Hey, rebuilding an orphanage is not my problem, mate,' he went on. 'Do I look like Bob Gandalf? TTFN.'

He hung up without saying goodbye and shot us with a finger pistol. 'The $OUN\slash D$ EXPERIENCE,' he said. 'Here at last.'

'What? We were two hours early!' said Ad. I trod on his foot to shut him up.

'The name's Jackson McHugh—A & R extraordinaire. Signed some of the biggest artists of this century. Oh, Inverted World, FTW, Mizz Gigglez. The bands in my portfolio have sold in excess of forty million records.'

He stared at us, as if he was expecting us to say something. No one did. I couldn't take it any more, so I went 'ooooh' as if I was at a panto.

'Damn straight,' said Jackson.

He has this really odd accent. English with a dollop of American. Like when he said, 'I was making a quarder of a mil a yerr before I was thirdy.'

He reached into his drawer and fanned out a pile of contracts. 'I have been given the *SOUND EXPERIENCE* as my own personal project. It's my job to mould you into superstars, just like I did with Marcy Slick.'

Wow, Marcy Slick. Now, that is impressive. She was the biggest pop star in the world. Until that incident.

Ad gasped. 'Is it true what they say about her?'

Jackson scowled. 'What do you mean?'

'You know . . . the goat.'

I coughed really loud. 'I think what Ad is trying to say is, we are very excited to work with someone with such an excellent track record.'

I glanced at Harry. He puffed on his pipe and gave me an approving nod.

Jackson pushed a pen across the table. 'I need you to sign. Then we can talk business.'

I picked up the pen. Harry put his hand on my arm. 'Don't you think we should read before we sign?'

Jackson chuckled. 'You're a sharp one. Read away—everything's above board.'

I picked up a contract and leafed through it. I nodded as if it all looked good to me, but I had NO IDEA what it said. Honestly, it was all 'the party' this and 'the party' that. It read like the world's most boring hip-hop song.

'Seems kosher,' I said.

I glanced at the guys—Ad was staring at a portrait of Marcy Slick with a quizzical look on his face, Harry was looking straight ahead, not giving anything away. Greeny was sneakily checking his phone for messages from Scott. I leaned over and quickly whacked him on the back of the head.

'Great,' said Jackson, flashing us a megawatt grin. 'Let's make it official.'

I hesitated. This was it—the thing they had been dreaming about for years. They were about to hit the big time. I was so happy for them. Especially Ad. I remember Mr Pratt telling him that the best job he could hope for was village idiot.

I took a deep breath and passed the contracts to them. The atmosphere was electric. We had done it. Signed with a major record label. It was such a proud moment, thinking back to their humble beginnings as mobile DJs, when

« Older posts

they didn't let everyone (mainly me) telling them they were terrible put them off.

'Now then.' Jackson leaned forward, his fingers in a pyramid. 'This is when the hard work starts. You might think that being pop stars is all limos and groupies, but you're wrong. It's blood, it's sweat, it's tears, it's graft. I've booked you some studio time for first thing tomorrow morning. Be there for seven, sharp.'

I think I heard Harry shriek slightly.

'We don't have long to get this record finished, so you're going to have to put the hours in. I'll be there with you for the first few sessions to make sure it all runs smoothly. Any questions?'

Greeny raised his hand. 'Do I have to be there? I mean, I just do the live projections and that.'

Jackson huffed and tapped the end of his pen on the desk. 'That's one of the changes we're bringing in. Get to our studio first thing tomorrow and I'll give you the full scoop then.'

'Wait a minute,' Greeny started, but Jackson interrupted.

'That'll be all, gents,' he said. 'I have a meeting with Marcy Slick's people in ten.'

'Is it about goats?' said Ad.

Jackson glowered at Ad, so I stood up and ushered them outside, saying, 'Thank you, see you tomorrow, looking forward to it,' the whole way.

When we left the building and walked out into the frosty air, Harry tapped me on the shoulder. 'What do you think he meant by "changes"?

'I wouldn't worry about it,' I said. 'It's probably nothing major.'

Tuesday 11th February

'Total. Overhaul.'

Jackson pounded his fist into his palm as he paced around the small office at the back of the studio.

'What does that mean?' I asked, clutching a horrible coffee that I hoped would keep me awake at this ungodly hour.

'You guys have potential,' he said. 'But potential doesn't shift units. We have to work with the raw material to find the diamond within.'

He blasted Greeny with a finger pistol. 'You're now the lead singer.'

'WHAT?' he cried.

'But we don't have a singer,' said Harry.

« Older posts

'Well you need one,' said Jackson. 'The days of the face-less dance duo are over. Do you think people buy records any more? Today it's all about touring, TV, and merch. And for that you need a focal point—someone to stick on the front cover of magazines. Greeny's the man.'

Greeny stared at me as if he was about to be gored in the goolies by an angry bull and I was the only one with a red rag.

'But, Jackson,' I said, 'Greeny isn't a frontman.'

Jackson turned on me, his mouth smiling, but his eyes pinprick furious. 'Well what is he doing on that video at *BUZZFEST*, then?'

He was referring to when Greeny came out on stage then sang 'Gay as the Day Is Long'.

'That was different,' said Greeny. 'It was spur of the moment. I can't do it all the time. Besides, who will do the projections?'

Jackson nodded. 'I hear what you're saying, but when you signed those contracts, you granted *PGS Records* complete control over the *SOUND EXPERIENCE* brand.'

'Brand?' said Ad. 'Don't you mean "band"?'

Jackson's eye twitched slightly. 'Listen, we don't have much time so I'm going to be blunt. I know what people want to see, I know what works, and, most importantly, I know what sells. What doesn't sell is projections. It's the type of thing that can be done automatically by a laptop.'

'No,' Greeny cried. 'It takes skill and timing.'

'This group needs a frontman and you are it. End of,' Jackson snapped.

Greeny's mouth dropped open. 'But I can't even sing!'

'That's why God invented autotune,' said Jackson.

We looked at each other. Harry chewed on his pipe so hard, I could hear the crunch.

'Oh and another thing,' Jackson went on. 'The SOUND EXPERIENCE is no good. Long names are out—one word names are in. From now on, you are XPERIENCE. Without an E.'

'Hold on a second, old boy,' said Harry. 'We didn't agree to any of this.'

'Yes you did,' said Jackson. 'When you signed that contract.'

'You said it was all above board,' Harry said to me.

Jackson held up his hands. 'You know, what you guys

« Older posts

are saying to me now, I've heard from every band I ever signed. When Marcy Slick first started, she wanted to go by her real name. And I said to her, "With all due respect, babe, no one is going to buy a record by Maureen Schlichtenberger now, are they?" Twenty million units later, here we are.'

'Didn't she check herself into rehab last year?' said Greeny.

'That's irrelevant,' said Jackson.

'An elephant?' said Ad. 'She moved on from goats pretty quick, didn't she?'

Jackson cut Ad off with a raised hand. 'I want you to do something for me—take all the energy you're expending on giving me a headache into the studio and make the best damn record you can.' His phone beeped. 'Ah, the producer is here.'

He led us into the control room overlooking the main studio. There was a massive bank of dials and buttons. Harry's and Ad's eyes darted around, taking it all in. They must have felt like I did when I visited the Star Trek museum.

'XPERIENCE,' said Jackson, 'meet your producer, Pepe Marisi.'

Harry and Ad stopped staring at the dials and looked straight at the bloke sitting at the desk.

'Oh,' said Harry. 'I . . . thought Buzz Algonquin was producing.'

The bloke at the desk, all long blond hair and orange tan, laughed and said, 'None taken, little dude.'

'Algonquin isn't a good fit for you,' said Jackson. 'Too artsy. What XPERIENCE need is someone more commercial, who will get us airplay. How many number one records have you produced, Pepe?'

'Too many,' Pepe drawled.

'We were promised Algonquin,' said Harry, jabbing with his pipe.

Jackson sighed and put his arm around Harry's shoulder. 'Listen, Gary. If you want to succeed in this industry, you have to roll with the punches and think outside the box. Pepe is perfect for you.'

'Wasn't his last song called "Bounce Your Bubble Butt"?' said Harry.

Pepe laughed. 'Took me ten minutes to write.'

'I can believe it,' said Harry.

Jackson squeezed his shoulder. 'What are you saying, guys?'

I stepped forward and whispered, 'I just think that the *SOUND EXP*— sorry, *XPERIENCE* are a little more sophisticated than Pepe's other collaborators.'

Jackson let go of Harry and slapped Pepe on the back. 'Sophisticated don't sell,' he said. 'Now let's go. Time is money.'

The three of them went into the studio and set the gear up. Greeny looked miserable. I tried to catch his eye through the thick glass, but he just stared at the floor the whole time.

Jackson clamped his hand on my shoulder. 'Look, I know morale's low now, but it'll pick up, it always does.'

I tried to believe him, but all these changes were going to be a shock.

'Is there anything I can do to make you guys happier?' he said. 'I mean, how are you getting on with your chaperone?'

I turned and looked at him. 'Um, not great.'

He nodded. 'Gleba is pretty hard core. Maybe too hard core for you guys. I assigned her to you because I thought you'd turn out to be party animals, but it looks like I was wrong on that score.'

'Oh, I don't know,' I said. 'I had quite a bit of fondue the other night.'

Jackson frowned at me, then continued, 'Well I've just had an offer from a new chaperone who wants to get in the game. He's way more chilled. I think you'll have fun with him.'

'OK,' I said. 'But what will happen to Mrs Gleba?'

'We've just signed a teen gangsta rap group, so I think they'd be a perfect fit,' he replied.

Can't argue with that.

Wednesday 12th February

The next day was much the same, and I left the studio at five to meet Mila. The guys stayed behind with Pepe, working on more tracks.

I'd like to say the recording sessions had been easy, but that would be a massive, stinking lie. Jackson kept interfering and telling them to change stuff. I mean, those songs are like their kids and he was telling them they were rubbish. You wouldn't go into someone's house and say, 'Your son stinks and your daughter looks like the back end of a yak,' would you?

When I told Mila, she was all, 'Oh I bet it's not that bad.'

'He's ruining their sound!' I said.

'Jackson knows what he's doing, Joe,' said Mila. 'I mean, look at his track record.'

We were in a fancy bar in Shoreditch. Mila was on her second glass of wine. I was on lemonade.

'He's got this Pepe bloke to write lyrics for the songs!' I said. 'They're awful. This one goes, "I love you like iOS loves updating." I mean, come on! Plus, Greeny has to sing them, and he sounds like a goose being strangled.'

Mila laughed and flicked my ear. 'You worry too much.'

'I do not,' I said. 'I worry just the right amount.'

She grabbed an olive out of a dish in the middle of the table. 'Open your mouth.'

I huffed. 'I don't like olives.'

'Open your mouth,' she urged, her big grey manga-character eyes drawing me in as they always do.

I did as I was told.

'If I get this olive in, XPERIENCE's album will go number one,' she said.

She took aim. It smacked off the end of my nose and landed in my drink.

'Oh dear,' I said.

'OK, we'll try again for number two,' she said.

She didn't manage that either. In the end, I think we got XPERIENCE's album to number twenty-five. Our table looked like an olive massacre.

When I got back up to the flat, I found Harry, Ad, and Greeny eating a chippy tea. That was weird. Mrs Gleba strictly outlawed chippy teas. She was always, 'Why spend money on greasy muck when I make you borsht for free?'

'She's gone, old son,' said Harry, through a mouthful of cod.

'What, that quick?' I said.

Greeny nodded. 'She went ten minutes ago. Didn't even get a kiss goodbye.'

I sat down at the table. 'So what happens now?'

'They're sending our new chaperone tonight,' said Ad. 'Should be here before ten.'

Ah, so this is that chilled bloke Jackson mentioned. I wonder if he'll be cool enough to get us back in with the penthouse set upstairs. Oh, hold on, I think he's here.

10 p.m.
No!

10.10 p.m.
No!

« Older posts

10.30 p.m.

NOOOOOOOOOOOOOOOOOOOOO!

12 a.m.

OK, I'm going to try to describe what happened now, but if the rest of the post is just a load of jumbled up letters, it's because I've resorted to headbutting the keyboard.

When the doorbell went, we all went to answer it together.

'I hope he's nicer than Mrs Gleba,' said Ad.

'Cripes, old son, a Rottweiler with appendicitis would be nicer than Mrs Gleba,' said Harry.

'Yeah,' I said. 'No matter who it is, he couldn't possibly be any worse.'

I opened the door.

'Wassup, homies?'

You know when people say they felt like all the air left their body? Well, I felt like that but a zillion times worse. Like my skeleton had left my body.

'DAD???!!!'

'Surprizzle!' he yelled. 'Guess who's your new C to the Cizzo, H to the Hizzay, A to the Azzo, P to the Pizzay . . .'

'Yes, chaperone—we get the

idea,' said Harry.

'Buh, buh, how? Why?' I gasped.

Dad chuckled. 'Well, I knew you'd be having a well rinsing time in the Smizzoke and I wanted to be part of it, so I got in touch with your record label and they agreed to let me be your C to the Cizzo, H to the . . .'

'Chaperone,' I said. 'You don't have to spell it with izzle letters every time.'

Dad strutted into the flat, dragging his Louis Vuitton suitcase behind him. 'Cool pad, yo! I bet the ladies love this crib.'

'But I don't get it,' I yammered. 'I mean, what about your job?'

Dad ran his hand over our marble worktop and whistled. 'It's all taken care of, G. I can work from home so my boss doesn't mind me being away from the office.'

'Can't imagine why,' said Harry.

'Mr Cowley?' said Ad.

Dad winked at him. ''Sup, Ad Rock?'

'What about your girlfriend?' Ad asked. 'What's her name? Satsuma?'

Dad smiled sadly. 'Svetlana. Yeah, me and Svet are going through a conscious uncoupling right now.'

Ad looked at me as if Dad was speaking Klingon.

'It means they split up.'

'Oh, why?' said Harry. 'Did your cheque to the Brides R

Us mail order company bounce?'

Greeny nearly spat out his health shake.

Dad playfully grabbed Harry and gave him a noogie. 'The bantz on this one. No, to be honest with you, homies, Svet and I just grew apart.'

'You mean she found out that you tried to gatecrash Mum's wedding,' I said.

Dad sighed and nodded. 'Quick tip for you playas. If you're going to hire a horse and carriage, don't pay on your credit card. Shows up on the statement.'

'Duly noted, old son,' said Harry. 'Anyway, we've got a long day in the studio tomorrow, so we should probably be turning in for the night.'

'What?' Dad cried. 'But it's not even half nine yet! We should be hitting the block, scopin' out the shawties!'

'I think they prefer to be called "small people", mate,' said Ad.

'Yes, we'll "hit the block" once our album is finished,' said Harry. And with that, the three of them headed for bed.

I should point out they each have their own room—they're not top-and-tailing.

'So, son,' said Dad once they'd gone. 'Looks like it's just you and me. So what do you say? Want to hit the town with your poppa?'

Ah crap. I didn't know what to do. I'm trying to reinvent myself as a cultured city boy, and I'm not going to do that with cocking Dadlemore tagging along with me.

'Oh, I would,' I said. 'But I promised my girlfriend I would go over to her flat.'

I promised no such thing. In fact, her dad doesn't want her bringing a boyfriend over, so it's pretty much impossible, but I wasn't about to admit that.

Dad winked at me. 'Booty call. Gotcha. Well, have fun, my li'l playa.'

And in a way, blog, I did have fun. I sat in an all-night cafe and made a single cup of tea last two hours.

Thursday 13th February

Another miserable day in the studio. I seemed to spend the whole time fetching coffee and something called keen-wah, which looks like food you'd only give to a budgie.

The guys seemed to be getting more miserable with every passing minute. When Jackson leaned into the control room mic and asked them to make it more 'Bieber-esque', I think I heard Harry's brain pop.

I'll say one thing, though. At least we weren't at the flat. I mean, is it wrong that I'm starting to miss Mrs Gleba? At least she made us breakfast in the morning. When we got up today, Dad was still in bed, having left a note saying:

I'll see y'all tonight. I'm laid up from too much partaying.

I must be adopted.

« Older posts

By the time we got back, after stopping off for salad (Greeny) and pizza (the rest of us), it was dark. I was about to switch the light on when Dad yelled for me to stop and I nearly crapped my pants.

'Why the hell are you standing in the dark?'

'Getting ready to turn and run,' said Greeny. 'In five . . . four . . . three . . .'

'While you guys were grinding in the studio, I took the liberty of pimping the crib,' he said.

Oh God.

'What do you mean?'

'Check this,' he said. 'If you're happy and you know it . . .'

None of us moved. I think if we were to make a list of the emotions we were feeling in that moment, happy would be twelve zillionth.

'Come on, my li'l hustlas, if you're happy and you know it . . .'

Nothing again.

'Fine,' Dad sighed, then clapped once. As soon as he did, the lights came on.

'What do you think? Pretty sweet or what?'

None of us said anything. Probably because we were distracted by the MASSIVE INFLATABLE HOT TUB RIGHT IN THE MIDDLE OF THE LIVING ROOM.

'You do know we have a landlord, right?' I said. I turned to the others for support, but Ad was already in his Y-fronts and halfway in.

'This place was already a sweet pad,' Dad said. 'It just needed a couple of extras to make it perfect.'

He switched on a massive pair of speakers and hip-hop started blaring out.

'Oh, for God's sake,' I said. 'Guys, we can't let this happen, can we?'

'Stop being a fanny and get in,' said Greeny, jumping in next to Ad.

'I don't get it, yo,' said Dad, sipping something called a mojito as he sat between me and Greeny in the tub. 'You guys are living the dream! Why do you look miserable?'

'It's the bloody record company, old son,' said Harry. 'They want to change everything about us.'

Dad shook his head as he swished the ice around in his

« Older posts

glass. 'That's crazy, yo. I remember watching you guys in that Buzzfest contest and you were wicked fresh.'

I wondered if I held his head under the water for long enough, he would become normal.

'Try telling them that,' said Harry. 'But we signed the contracts so we're stuck.'

No one said anything for a while. I couldn't believe we were so excited to be signing that contract just a few days ago.

Dad clicked his fingers. 'Hold on a minute. Those chicas of yours, don't their folks work for the record company?'

'Yeah,' said Ad.

'So why don't you talk to them? See if they can pull a few strings?'

We all looked at each other uneasily.

'As shocked as I am to say it, that's a pretty good idea,' said Harry.

'Hey,' Dad said. 'Just cos I look superfly don't mean I ain't got it going on upstairs.'

'I've already tried talking to Mila, but I didn't really get anywhere,' I said.

Harry grabbed the laptop and balanced it on the floating drinks tray. 'Never mind. Joe is far too whipped to make an impact. We can Skype Verity and Jasmeen in Italy now. Ad, scooch closer.'

'Now then,' Harry went on. 'We have to be strong. Tell

them to get their dads to reassign that buffoon McHugh, and to hire Algonquin to produce our album, which we are NOT naming "The Three Dancemen of the HipHopalypse".'

The call connected. I leaned over to get a closer look. Verity and Jasmeen popped up on the screen.

'Hey, guys,' they said, together.

'Greetings, my love,' said Harry. 'How wonderful to see your beautiful face.' It's funny watching him talk to Verity. His stiff-upper-lip-keep-calm-and-carry-on-I'm-Winston-Churchill routine goes right out of the window.

Verity smiled softly. 'You know PGS pay the bills right? You don't have to take baths together.'

'This ain't a bath, it's a hot tub,' said Ad.

'What's the difference?' said Verity.

None of us could come up with anything. All of a sudden, I felt super uncomfortable.

'Anyway, Jas,' said Ad. 'How's Europe and that?'

'Oh, we're having the best time,' said Jasmeen. 'We've met some really cool people, too. How are you guys?'

'Actually, that's what we wanted to speak to you about,'

« Older posts

said Harry. 'We are having some issues with PGS.'

'What kind of issues?' said Verity.

'They're changing our name, our sound, everything,' said Harry. 'They're destroying what we created.'

'Did you sign a contract?' said Jasmeen.

'Well, yeah,' said Ad.

'Then there's not a lot you can do,' she said. 'Just trust them. It might seem weird to begin with, but they know what they're doing.'

'Jas is right,' said Verity. 'I promise, you're in good hands.'

'But—'

'I'm serious—you'll be fine,' said Verity. 'Anyway, we've got to go. We're meeting the boys at the bar in ten. Ciao!'

The feed went silent. All we could hear was the quiet bubbling of the tub.

'So,' said Greeny. 'Who do you think these boys are, then?'

Harry growled and slammed the laptop shut with a loud bang that made all the lights go out.

Friday 14th February

Another day, another miserable recording session. Greeny was nearly in tears by lunchtime because he kept getting the words wrong and Pepe and Jackson wouldn't let it go. In the end, he had to have a FaceTime pep talk from Scott before he could continue.

With everything that has been happening, I had completely forgotten it was Valentine's Day. I tried to book a table at a restaurant but the woman on the phone laughed at me and hung up. Luckily, Mila was OK with just coming over tonight to watch a film. I wasn't too happy about that, what with Dad and his 'improvements'. I mean, for one thing, that clap light is too sensitive. Last night, Ad did a rapid-fire series of mini farts and it was like a disco in there.

I had a quick look through the what's on listings and saw that someone called MC Brady was playing at a pub a couple of minutes from the flat. I texted Dad the details, telling him I'd heard through my contacts that he was 'wicked fresh'. Ugh, my thumbs felt dirty just typing it.

When Mila arrived, I gave her a hug and said, 'Happy Valentine's Day!' which made her laugh.

'What's so funny?'

'You're being ironic, right?' she said. 'Valentine's Day is so lame.'

I tried to laugh but what came out sounded more like a chipmunk in a blender. 'Of course,' I said. 'Ironic. That's what I was being.'

I made a mental note to go to my room and hide the balloons, flowers, chocolates, and oversized novelty card complete with personalized poem.

« Older posts

> Mila, Mila,
> I like you so much.
> Mila, Mila,
> You are Dutch.

Yeah, I could have spent a bit more time on that one.

The film was one of those subtitled dealies about a French bloke who stands on bridges and smokes. It was proper boring, but I pretended to like it because I didn't want to seem like a moron in front of Mila. When Frenchie stared into the distance with a sad look in his eyes, I would say stuff like 'intense' and 'moving' and 'what a nice bridge'. Then Mila would snuggle up closer to me and say how great it is to be dating someone so sensitive.

It would have been better if it weren't for Harry, Ad, and Greeny sitting in the hot tub next to us, stewing in their own juices, but there we go.

'So what's this film about, anyway?' Ad asked Mila, leaning over the side. 'When do the explosions start?'

Mila laughed. 'There are no explosions, Ad. It is an exploration of the idea of finding God in a godless world.'

This was news to me, but I wasn't about to let on.

'Quite,' I said.

'I saw the face of God in a window, once,' said Ad.

'Really?' said Mila, sitting up.

'You were in a church, old son,' said Harry. 'It was a

stained-glass window.'

'Oh yeah.'

I sneakily checked my phone. I had to do something. The film was boring me to tears. I felt like screaming, 'WHY DON'T YOU TRY LOOKING FOR GOD DOWN THE BACK OF THE SOFA, PIERRE?'

A little red '1' was in the corner of the mail envelope. I tutted. Getting emails set up on my phone was the worst mistake I ever made. I'm constantly deleting messages from pretend women who want to have pretend 'fun times' with me. Fun times that generally involve me giving them my bank details.

I clicked my inbox and my thumb started its usual journey to the delete button, but then it stopped.

FROM: Natalie Tuft
TO: Joe Cowley
SUBJECT: Hi

WHAT? I started choking on the chip I was eating. Mila whacked me on the back a couple of times and dislodged it. When I went into the kitchen to get a glass of water, I checked again. It was still there. I hadn't dreamt it.

I leaned on the counter and tried to compose myself. Yes, Natalie was my first love, my best friend, my soulmate, blah, blah, blah, but that is all over now. She ended it with me when I kissed Lisa Hall, and despite all my attempts to get her back, she's happier without me.

SO WHY DID SHE EMAIL ME?

A bright light flashed in my head. Dials whirred into life; machines that had lain dormant for months started to click and beep.

The control room awoke.

Well, look who's come crawling back, said Hank, folding his arms. *What's the matter? Is the big city boy not so big after all? Has he finally accepted the fact that he's a freakin' wuss who misses his MOMMY?*

Now, now, Hank, said Norman. *It is a good thing that Joe has been able to cope without us for such a long time. It shows he's growing as a person. Now, I believe the problem we are faced with is that he doesn't know whether to read the email from Natalie.*

Another control room worker ran over to them. *His confusion levels are off the charts. He's trying to remind him-*

self how happy he is with Mila, but memories of Natalie are
leaving the vaults quicker than we can stop them.

Norman leaned on the control panel. *Until Joe reads the*
email, we're not going to know what we're dealing with. I
would advise taking a peek. It's probably nothing to worry
about.

Dude, are you shaking? said Hank.

I took a deep breath and clicked on it. As soon as I did, I
switched my phone to standby and threw it onto the counter. What was wrong with me? Why couldn't I read a simple
email from my ex-girlfriend? I mean, maybe she'd just been
hacked and was sending out spam for willy pills? Yeah, that
was it.

I picked my phone back up, counted to ten and looked
at the screen.

Hey Cowley (I've decided that's what I'm calling
you now, hope that's cool!),

Just thought I'd get in touch and see how you're
getting on in London. I want to hear all the Sound
Experience gossip. I was hoping Greeny would be my
line on that, but he's all 'Whatever, Nat, you're not
Scott, so jog on.' Unbelievable.

So, how's things with Mila? Haven't driven her crazy

« <u>Older posts</u>

yet, have you?

Things are the same as ever here. Mad Morris is still mad, my parents are still annoying, Griddler's chips still give me heartburn. The only thing that's changed is . . . (epic drumroll) . . . I HAVE PASSED MY DRIVING TEST! I am a motorist! Can you believe it?

I even have my own parking space at college. Makes me feel like a real big shot. College is pretty different from school, btw. You can call teachers by their first names, and people have debates about stuff like politics rather than who left that turd in Mr Pratt's drawer. I'm doing Psychology, Biology, and Chemistry A levels, which bend my head something rotten but . . .

Ugh, you know something, Cowley? I miss you. All of you. I had my music on shuffle the other day and Kamikaze Attack came on, and it just made me realize how much I bloody well miss you. So, you have to keep in touch, OK? OK??????

Love,
Nat
PS I secretly hope you're having a HORRIBLE time without me.

'What are you reading?'

Mila squeezed my sides, and I jumped so high, I whacked my head on the extractor fan.

'Oh, just an email,' I squeaked, rubbing my throbbing skull. 'Nothing important.'

Mila laughed and picked up a drink. 'You're such a klutz. Anyway, hurry back, Renoir is about to say something pro-found again.'

A twinge of guilt made me wince. How could I get so excited about Natalie when I have a brilliant girlfriend who wants to snuggle with me and watch crappy French mov-ies?

I decided to wait a while before I responded, but the con-trol room was non-stop action, drafting and redrafting my reply until it stopped making sense.

 The feeling we have in the back, said one of the workers, *is that we should go with a polite, measured response. Let her know what's happening but don't get too personal.*

Norman nodded and rubbed his chin. *I don't think we should rule out the personal quite so quickly. It is possible to do so without crossing into difficult territory.*

Guys, Hank interrupted, leaning back in his chair. *We're overthinking this. Just write 'Wassup, sweet cheeks, do you have the hots for me again, or what?'*

'So, what did you think of that?'

I jumped again. Mila's face was right in front of mine.

« Older posts

'Um, yeah. Yeah. Very . . . French. *J'ai fini mon cahier.*'

Mila poked me in the stomach. 'What's the matter with you tonight, Joe? You've been really quiet.'

I shook my head. 'Nothing. I'm fine. Just thinking . . . about that . . . film.'

Mila laughed. 'It was kind of depressing, wasn't it? I mean, God never showed up. I guess he must have been busy. Hey, I've thought of something that might cheer you up.'

'Really?' I said. 'What?'

Before she could tell me, the door opened and Dad burst in.

''Sup, homeboys and, ooh, homegirls.' He stopped in front of Mila. 'How you doin, shawty? You must be Mila. Pleasure to meet you. In case you were wondering where Joe got his good looks, look no further.'

Mila giggled. 'So you're Joe's dad?'

Dad doffed his Ed Hardy cap. 'It's hard to believe that someone as young as me could have a sixteen-year-old son, but that's right, babe.'

Christ, he just called her babe, said Hank. *We need to do something.*

'Soooo,' I said. 'How was the show?'

Dad plonked himself into a chair. 'Well, bro, it seems there was a misunderstanding,' he said. 'It wasn't MC Brady the rapper, it was McBrady, the Irish folk singer.'

Oh God, I hope he wasn't freestyling over the top of it.

'Do you not like Irish music, Mr Cowley?' Mila asked.

Dad smiled, his gold tooth glinting in the light. 'Please, call me Keith. Or better yet, K-Dawg. And no, Irish music ain't my scene. Irish chicas on the other hand . . .' He stopped and made a pistol cocking gesture. 'Yow. I was trying to get the digits of this fine honey at the bar, but she wasn't giving them up easy.'

Oh God. Chicas. Digits. Why can't he just be normal? With the as-yet-unreplied-to email from Natalie burning a hole in my pocket, this was the last thing I needed.

'So are you on the market again, old son?' said Harry.

Dad nodded. 'A man has needs, you know?'

I facepalmed. 'Oh, can you not?'

'What's the matter, son?' said Dad. 'Just because I'm your dad doesn't mean I'm not a hot-blooded being with certain needs.'

'Ughhh, I think I'm going to vom,' I groaned over Harry's, Ad's, and Greeny's shrieks of laughter.

'It's true, dawg,' Dad said. 'And let me tell you who was really dynamite in that department—your mother.'

The control room burst into action.

Quick, shut down the mental image sector before we go into meltdown!

« Older posts

'I knew it!' said Ad.

By this point, even Mila was laughing.

After I'd walked her to the door, I went straight back to my room and got my laptop out. I needed maximum concentration and I wasn't going to get it in the lounge, where Dad was scouring dating sites and asking Greeny to rate the women out of ten (barking up the wrong tree, there), and Harry and Ad were throwing things at Crocodile Dundee playing on the TV.

After obsessively honing and refining, I finally hit send at 3 a.m. Here's what I ended up with.

Hi, Tuft (actually, that sounds awful—I'll stick to Natalie),

It's really great to hear from you, and I'm glad you're doing well.

The Sound Experience stuff is going . . . fine. OK, maybe not fine. To be honest, we're having a few 'creative differences' with the label:

- They're now called 'Xperience'.
- They're making Greeny be the lead singer.
- They're totally changing their sound.

So basically, they're now a completely different band.

Things are fine with Mila, too.

Anyway, it was really cool to hear from you,
Joe
PS I think it's great that we can talk like this now. You know, without me being a total moron.
PPS And I miss you, too.
PPPS And sometimes, when I think about you, I want to cry.

I deleted all the PSs.

Saturday 15th February

You might think, it being a Saturday, that Jackson would give us a day off from recording. Well, you'd think wrong, my friend. He had us back in there at eight o'clock sharp.

I was already in a bad mood because the dishwasher hadn't been unloaded so there was about three days' washing up by the sink and of course I ended up doing it. I mean, the lengths the others had been going to to get around it was ridiculous. I walked in on Greeny drinking Diet Coke out of an egg cup, for God's sake. AND we need

« Older posts

more shopping and I bet I'll be the one who has to do it. If Ad goes, who knows what we'll end up with.

When we got to the studio, I sat in one of the comfy chairs in the control room. After a while I must have dropped off, because the next thing I know, I'm woken up by:

'NO! THAT IS ENOUGH, DO YOU HEAR ME? ENOUGH!'

It was Harry, and he looked like he was doing his nut.

Jackson pressed a button and spoke into a mic on the mixing desk.

'Sorry, but we have to lose all those air raid sirens,' he said. 'World War Two just isn't sexy,' he said.

Harry stomped out from behind his keyboard and pointed up at the control room. 'One, how can you have a song called Kamikaze Attack without air raid sirens, and two, NOBODY SAID WORLD WAR TWO WAS SUPPOSED TO BE SEXY. NOT EVERYTHING HAS TO BE SEXY, YOU THUNDERING BUFFOON!'

Harry was tetchy because Verity wasn't replying to his texts and Jackson's constant interfering was only making him worse.

'How about you boys?' Jackson said to Ad and Greeny.

'I agree with Harry,' said Ad, glumly.

'Me too,' said Greeny. 'And I think it would be even better without me singing over the top of it—I mean these lyrics are shocking—"your love melts my heart like jet fuel can't melt steel beams"? I only managed a C in English but even

I know that makes no sense.'

'The lyrics are non-negotiable,' said Jackson. 'Now let's try it again. Take thirty-seven.'

When they started up again, their playing was even better. I began to think that maybe Jackson was deliberately antagonizing the boys to get the best out of them.

Or maybe he's just a knob.

While they were playing, I checked my phone. Another email from Natalie.

Shields up, said Norman.

Cowley!

That sucks! I thought you were their manager! You need to manage this!

I KNEW I should have come with you.

Have a word with them.

Actually, it's you I'm talking to. Carefully plan what you're going to say first. And I mean CAREFULLY. Under no circumstances should you adlib. Remember that time we ran into my Auntie Teresa in town and you noticed she only had two fingers on one hand, and you said something about how easy she would be to

« Older posts

beat at Rock, Paper, Scissors? God, I'm crying laughing, just thinking about it.

Let me know how it goes, Cowley.

Nat x

That's what I'm going to have to do, I thought. Confront him head on. Before I could prepare a speech, though, I was interrupted by Jackson standing over me.

'Is there something more important on that phone than your job?' he said.

'N-no.'

'Good,' he shot back. 'Because you are here to learn from the best. And to fetch the best drinks. Mine will be an Americano, and try to make it quicker this time.'

I took a deep breath. 'Actually, Jackson, there is something I need to talk to you about.'

Jackson frowned, then pulled a chair from the control panel and sat on it backwards like some kind of cowboy. 'Shoot.'

Hold on! Hank cried. *You didn't give us time to prepare!*

'Um, well, the thing is . . .' I looked into his eyes but they were narrow and piercing like a viper and I had to look away before he pounced and sunk his fangs into my jugular. 'I have some, erm, issues with the . . . what do you call it? Creative direction of the band. And I wanted to address them with you.'

I stopped and looked at him. His expression hadn't changed.

'I-I just think we're going too far from what made them good. And Greeny isn't a frontman. I mean, he both sings and dances like a dying walrus. And I—'

Jackson cut me off with a raised palm. 'So what are we saying, Joe?'

What are we saying? said Hank.

Norman shuffled some papers then sighed and said, *I don't know.*

'I-I'm saying that maybe you-you-you've got it w-wrong?'

Jackson glared at me. His snake eyes burned through me. I bet this is what meeting the Devil feels like.

After what felt like about seven years, he laughed. 'I like your style, Joe. You're looking after your boys and I've got a lot of time for that.'

Wow, that went better than I thought, said Hank.

'OK,' I said. 'So are you going to change them back?'

Jackson laughed again, this time louder. 'Oh Lord no. When it comes to XPERIENCE, no one knows them better than Jackson Xavier McHugh. But I have big plans for you, Joe. As of next week, I'm splitting you up. The lads will stay here and you'll come with me back to the office.'

I gulped. 'Um, OK. So what will I be doing there?'

« Older posts

'Learning the ropes, my friend,' he said.

That sounded interesting. I mean, maybe he'll give me a chance to make some real decisions. Then I can earn his trust and be given a shot at managing XPERIENCE's career. Who knows, by the time we get around to their next album, I could be the one calling the shots.

Yes, that is going to be my mission, and I am definitely going to make it happen.

Kid never learns, does he? said Hank.

Sunday 16th February

Picture the scene, blog. It's eight o'clock on Saturday night and we're only just getting in from a thirteen-hour day. We're exhausted, we're tetchy, we just want to crawl into bed and forget about everything.

But when we walk in, a middle-aged man who claims to be my biological father is standing there, saying, 'Don't sit down, bros, the limo will be here any minute.'

Have you pictured it? Good. Now are you glad you are an insentient collection of computer code? I envy you, blog, I really do.

'Limo?' I groaned.

Dad grabbed us all in a huddle.

'You know why I came here to hang with you playas?'

Harry shrugged. 'Some sort of life crisis?'

'Grandmaster Haz,' Dad chuckled. 'Always busting my

chops. No, I came to the Big Smizzoke because I knew that someone was going to have to teach you boys how to partay.'

I tried to make eye contact with the other guys to show how sorry I was, but they were all looking at Dad like an old lady looks at a mugger.

'Honestly, Dad, it's fine,' I said. 'We partay enough.'

'That's not what I heard, yo,' he said.

'What's that supposed to mean?' said Harry.

Dad leaned closer to me, which was horrible because he smelled like he'd marinated himself in nasty cologne.

'I was talking to those fine chicas from the penthouse and they told me that your old chaperone dragged you out of their partay by your ears.'

God, what a pair of blabbers.

'Honestly, Keith,' said Greeny.

Dad stopped him. 'I told you, G-Solja, we're bros now. Call me K-Dawg.'

'Honestly, Keith,' said Greeny. 'We're knackered. Maybe we'll go out some other time.'

Dad shook his head. 'No way—the limo's booked, yo! Besides, you guys need to get out there and live! You're here in the best city in the world and you're wasting your nights watching season five of *Game of Thrones*, even though everyone knows that Jon Snow dies in the last episode.'

« Older posts

'You MONSTER,' Harry hissed.

'Come on,' said Dad. 'I'll show you the night of your life, you just wait.'

His phone beeped.

'Looks like the limo's here, y'aaallllll!' Then he clapped and all the lights went out.

When we got downstairs, we found it wasn't just a limo, it was a stretch Hummer. I mean, it was totally ridiculous.

'Look at this bitchin'-ass ride!' Dad yelled.

I kept my head down and got in. People were staring.

I knew Mila was out with some friends at a bar near her house called Kahuna's, so I asked the driver to take us there.

'Kahuna's,' said Dad, mixing himself a cocktail. 'Sounds wicked fresh.'

I had no idea whether it was wicked or indeed fresh as

I'd never been before, but I knew if Mila was there, I'd be able to lose Dad for the night. A foolproof plan. I texted her to let her know I was on the way. She said she'd look out for me.

When we arrived, there was a queue outside stretching around the corner, and the door was being guarded by a massive bouncer.

People were staring at the Hummer. They probably thought we were celebrities.

'Right, dawgs,' said Dad. 'I know you playas ain't quite eighteen yet, so we might have to get jiggy with the truth, you know what I'm saying?'

'I want a kebab,' said Ad.

Dad drained the last of his cocktail and leaned forward. 'If they ask you your date of birth, use your normal birthday, but change the year to 1998, you got that?'

I nodded, keen to find Mila and escape Dad. The last thing I wanted was to be forced into some kind of dance-off.

I got out first to the sound of a hundred people sighing with disappointment.

'I don't know who he is.'

'Maybe he's on *Made in Chelsea*.'

'Nah, I think he was in the *Countdown* final.'

I went to head to the back of the queue, but Dad grabbed me and marched straight up to the bouncers. The four of us skulked behind him.

« Older posts

''Sup brother,' he said to the bouncer, making my toes curl so hard, they almost disappeared into my feet. 'You gonna let us in, right?'

The bouncer's massive Easter Island face creased into a frown. 'When you get to the back of the line. Maybe.'

Dad glanced at us and laughed. 'You're kidding me. Do you know these guys are the hottest new thing in music? They're signed to VHS.'

'PGS,' said Harry.

'PGS,' said Dad.

The bouncer gave him an I-can't-be-arsed-with-this eye-roll and scratched his head. 'Right, fine, you're in.'

'I can't believe that worked,' Harry muttered.

I looked into the bar and could see Mila near the door, waiting for me. She smiled and waved. That was when I felt the hand of death on my shoulder.

'Wait a minute,' said the bouncer. 'I'm going to need to see some ID.'

Dad chuckled and smoothed down his goatee. 'I'm flattered, bro, but I'm actually the wrong side of forty. Hard to believe, I know.'

'Not you, them,' he said, pointing a baton finger at us.

I swear, I thought my knees were going to start knocking together. This bloke was the size of Galactus.

'See, here's the deal, yo,' said Dad. 'The boys had to send their ID to the record company. They won't let them keep it in case they get ID thefted. Don't believe me, you can call Jackson McDonald and ask him.'

'McHugh,' said Harry.

'Bless you,' said Dad. 'So come on, playa, are we in or are we in?'

The bouncer narrowed his eyes at Ad. 'You. What's your date of birth?'

NO! Hank screamed. *OUT OF ALL OF THEM WHY DID YOU HAVE TO ASK HIM?*

I leaned closer to Ad and said, 'Remember what Dad told you.'

Ad nodded. 'Yeah,' he said. 'It's the thirteenth of October

. . . 19 . . . 38.'

Hank threw himself to the floor and pounded it with his fists.

'Wow,' said the bouncer. 'You look good considering you're nearly eighty.'

'Aw thanks, mate!' said Ad.

I facepalmed.

'Out,' said the bouncer. 'Now.'

We went to leave but Dad stopped us. 'Woah, let's be cool, yo. No need to be straight tripping, you feel me?'

Mila was still watching, but looked worried now.

Dad reached into his pocket, then shook the bouncer's hand. 'I'm sure us ballas can come to some kind of arrangement.'

The bouncer looked at his hand, then back at Dad. 'Are you trying to bribe me?'

Dad laughed. 'When you say it like that, you make it sound salty, dawg.'

The bouncer looked at me as if to say, 'Where the

cocking hell did you find this moron?' Then said, 'If you're going to try to pay me off, it'll take more than a fiver.'

'All right, G,' said Dad, rummaging around in his wallet. 'I've got eight pounds . . . seventy . . . three.'

'Well, old son,' said Harry as we pulled away, 'thanks for teaching us how to partay.'

Dad shook his head. 'You think I'd be so whack as to take you out with no backup plan?' He scooted over to the hatch and passed the driver a slip of paper.

'Ad,' I whispered, 'try the door.'

He yanked at the handle. 'It's locked.'

'Damn.'

My phone beeped—a text from Mila.

What happened? X

I thought about lying—telling her that the bouncer thought we looked too sophisticated and would put their regular clientele to shame. But I couldn't bring myself to do it.

They wouldn't let us in cos we didn't have ID and Ad told them he was an OAP.

You know, I don't think honesty is always the best policy.

Looking through the tinted windows, I noticed the streets getting progressively grimier. There were less fancy wine bars and more shops with names like Exotic Massageland and XXX Secretz and Londis.

« Older posts

'Where are we going?' I asked Dad.

'Chillax,' said Dad, helping himself to another cocktail. 'The place we're headed has a more authentic vibe. We're gonna mix with real London peeps.'

Harry gasped. 'He's taking us to a cockfighting tournament, isn't he?'

'That sounds well disgusting,' said Ad.

By the time we'd explained to Ad what cockfighting actually was, we were there. It wasn't that, though. It was way worse.

'It's even more dope than I dreamed, y'all,' said Dad.

'Question,' said Harry, looking at what was basically a warehouse with ear-explodingly loud music blasting out of it. 'By "dope" do you mean "hellish"?'

'I'll show you,' said Dad. 'Come on, let's get all up in there.'

I thought about running. I mean, I had no idea where I was but I could figure it out. Maybe I could ask someone for directions . . . that tramp accusing a wheelie bin of assassinating President Kennedy looked helpful. Or maybe that gang loitering in the alley.

Damn. I was really going to have to go in, wasn't I?

The warehouse was rammed. A DJ was playing hardcore gangsta rap on a stage at the far end. Harry and Ad nodded appreciatively. I couldn't help but feel uneasy, though. People were looking at us weirdly. I don't know why—I mean, don't they get many people in *'What Would Picard Do?'* T-shirts at rap clubs? Someone actually went up to Harry and asked him where he got that retro e-cig.

Plus, Dad wasn't exactly being incon-cocking-spicuous, grabbing his medallion and throwing gang signs all over the place.

'All right, people,' said the DJ over the mic. 'It's time for the next round. Give it up for Dropzy and Killer P.'

The crowd cheered and whooped as these two women in tracksuits got up on stage and grabbed mics.

'Represent, sistas!' Dad yelled.

Loads of people stared at him and I prayed to Jesus, Mary, Joseph, and basically the entire cast of the Nativity play that no one would find out he was my dad.

The DJ played a beat, then one of the rappers, let's say it was Dropzy, started spitting out rhymes about how great she was and how crappy the other one was. When she finished, everyone cheered, and I'm pretty sure my dad shouted, 'Oh no she dittint!'

Then it was Killer P's turn, and she was even more vicious, saying nasty things about Dropzy's rap skills, hair, and grandma. It was brutal, but people were loving it.

When she was done, the DJ got the crowd to cheer for who they liked best. The reaction for Killer P was louder, so she was declared the winner.

I turned to see what the guys thought of it all. Harry and

Ad looked like they were really into it. Greeny was on the phone to Scott, shouting something about how he'd been forced to go to a rap battle with the most embarrassing man in the world.

What's weird is that I felt a bit offended by that. I mean, yeah, my dad's embarrassing, but he can't be the worst in the world.

'Moving on, give it up for Heavy Def!' the DJ said.

The crowd exploded and chanted his name. This Heavy Def must have been a big deal. And he was a big everything else, too. He was like the Hulk in Adidas.

'Now, we got a bit of a problem, Def,' said the DJ when the cheering died down.

'Oh yeah, what's that?' he replied.

'Well, when your opponent heard he was going to be battling you, he did a runner, bruv.'

The crowd laughed and hooted.

'Can't blame him,' said Heavy Def. 'But I got rhymes to spit and I gotta get them out. So I'm issuing an open challenge. Anyone who's got the guts to face me, step up.'

I looked around to see if anyone was going to challenge him, but they were all rooted to the spot. No one was going to be stupid enough to take on this behemoth. I turned to Dad to see what he thought.

But he wasn't there.

'Wassuuuuuuuuuup, homeboys and homegirls!'

We have a Dad-related situation in progress, said Norman. *Code red, this is not a drill.*

With vibrations of nausea and horror coursing through my body, I watched my dad strike ridiculous poses onstage.

No, this could not be happening. Maybe I fell asleep in the Hummer and this was all a horrific nightmare.

'All the honeys in the house say "ooh ooh"!'

Silence. Like, you could almost hear crickets.

You need to stop him, Joe, said Norman. *Get up there and talk him down.*

And have all these people know that he is his son? said

« Older posts

Hank. *Are you freakin' crazy?*

'Riiiiight,' said the DJ, clearly a gnat's pube from laughing his arse off. 'What's your name, bro?'

Dad laughed. 'I'll save it for my rhyme.'

The DJ chuckled and said, 'All right. Up first, it's Heavy Def.'

He played a beat and Heavy Def totally ripped into Dad. He said something about him being a granddad who had a colostomy bag, which made the crowd cheer so loud, it rattled the pigeon-crap-caked rafters. I mean, imagine if Dad had a colostomy bag. He'd probably 'pimp' it by sticking diamonds on it and installing a set of speakers.

While all this was happening, Dad stood there with his arms folded and his legs really far apart. I think he was trying to look gangsta, but actually, he just looked like his ball sack was stuck to his leg.

When Heavy Def had finished and the crowd finally stopped cheering, the DJ sighed and went, 'And in the other corner—this bloke.'

The beat kicked in and Dad strode to the front of the stage.

'Put your hands in the air, London!' he yelled.

Every arm stuck to every side.

Now, blog, I am going to transcribe exactly how his rap went. You might be wondering how I remembered it. Well let's just say that the embarrassment was so acute that it will be forever in my brain as if branded there with a scalding hot iron.

> *'Sup, 'sup, 'sup.*
> *Well, my name's K-Dawg and I'm here to say,*
> *This rap game needs more positivitay.*
> *I ain't gonna flame my boy Heavy Def,*
> *Imma just give him props . . .*
> *Ooooooooh, treble clef.*

> *Said I'm K-Dawg and I want y'all to know,*
> *That I bring joy wherever I go,*
> *Ooh, what rhymes with go?*
> *Joe! Joe rhymes with go!*
> *Joe is my son and he's standing over there.*
> *Wearing a Star Trek T-shirt and he . . . has . . . hair.*
> *I'm so proud I impregnated his mum,*
> *And that he shot out of her tum.*
> *K-Dawg out.*

Then he dropped the mic and it made a horrible squealing sound.

The beat stopped only to be replaced by the loudest boo anyone has ever heard ever.

'Yeah, thanks, K-Dawg,' said the DJ. 'Well I think it's safe to say Heavy Def won that one.'

Dad went to protest, but the booing got so loud, it almost became a physical object designed to get him the hell off the stage.

When we got back in the Hummer, no one knew what to say. Except Dad.

'That was rinsing, yo!'

We all looked at each other, probably wondering if we could get the driver to drop him off at the nearest asylum.

'Um, you are aware how that actually went aren't you, old son?' Harry asked.

Dad laughed. 'Hey, I know I didn't exactly burn that hizzouse down, but that ain't the point.'

'So what was the point, then?' I asked.

'Point is, I did it, man,' said Dad. 'For the first time in my life, I'm really living. And it's all thanks to you playas. Trust. I'm never leaving. Imma chaperone you forever.'

'I feel sick,' said Ad.

I know how he felt.

Monday 17th February

First day interning at PGS today. We were all up together because the rest of the guys were back in the studio first thing. Apparently, today they were having another go at Greeny's rap verse. They'd attempted it forty times on Saturday and Greeny ended up screaming obscenities at Pepe and putting his foot through a drum.

I ironed my suit and spent an hour in front of the mirror getting my hair just right. Well, as just right as my hair gets.

There was only a tiny bit of toothpaste left, so I had to roll the tube up proper tight and squeeze the last dregs out.

'Someone's looking grown-up,' said Greeny when I finally emerged.

'Got to make a good impression on my first day,' I said.

'Quite right,' said Harry. 'We need you in there, fighting our corner. See if you can get the ear of the chairman.'

'Don't see how that's going to help,' said Ad, munching on Marmite on toast. 'I mean, what are we going to do with some bloke's chopped-off earhole?'

Harry shook his head and said, 'I mean it. Game face on, Private Cowley. Let's not have a repeat of the time you came to my fancy dress party and ended up crying for your mummy.'

« Older posts

'One,' I said, counting off on my fingers, 'I was six, so that doesn't count. And two, I was dressed as Batman, so I was actually just getting into character.'

Anyway, I tried to remember the whole stay-strong thing when I arrived at PGS, but inside I felt anything but. I mean, here I was, working for one of the biggest record companies in the world with a CV that looks like this:

Joseph Marvin Cowley
CURRICULUM VITAE

Paper boy (1.5 days): Delivered papers. Got chased by Blenkinsop twins.

Meat van assistant (1 day): Helped sell meat. Called old lady a thieving cow.

Roadkill scraper (3 days): Scraped roadkill. Puked.

SOUND EXPERIENCE manager: Didn't understand their music. Helped them to second place in a contest, just to spite this knobber called Seb. Accidentally ruined their gimmick and nearly wrecked their career.

'You've done a decent job with the SOUND EXPERIENCE,' said Jackson after I was led to his office by his secretary.

He was sitting in his massive chair, his eyes hidden behind a pair of expensive-looking aviators. 'That gay gimmick— wow. And the scene you made at *BUZZFEST* was some next-level stuff. But PR is only part of the job. You are going to be learning the ropes, seeing how I do it. Then, who knows? One day you might be sitting here.' He pointed downwards with both hands.

I gasped. 'In your lap?'

His smile disappeared. 'No, in my chair. Do you have any idea how much scratch I make per annum?'

I shook my head.

'More than you've ever seen in your life,' he said, with a crocodile grin. 'Chelsea apartment, place in NYC, holidays in the Bahamas—sound good to you?'

God, it does. Imagine having your own swanky place. No Greeny leaving his protein shakes everywhere, no Harry putting up World War Two posters, no having to get up in

« Older posts

the night to stop Ad trying to sleepwalk out of the window in his birthday suit, and most importantly, NO DAD.

Me and Mila could be international jetsetters and everything. And I would do things differently if I was in charge—I would let artists stay true to themselves, not change them to fit the latest fads. Yes, I am going to be the best A & R man ever.

'Sounds great,' I said.

'That's what I like to hear,' he said. 'Mine'll be a mac-chiato. Kitchen's down the hall.'

Tuesday 18th February

So that was me learning the ropes. Making coffee in a slightly different location. I might as well be one of those *Starbucks* batistas or whatever they're called.

Anyway, today was more of the same—taking coffee orders from Jackson and the various weirdoes that trooped into his office, and occasionally checking my phone to see WhatsApps from Harry, complaining that Pepe is making them replace machine-gun noises with air horns.

The only difference was, I ran into Mila on the corridor.

'Oh hey, Joe, I was hoping I'd see you today!' she said. I noticed she was holding a cup of coffee identical to mine.

'Hi, Mila,' I said. 'Are you visiting your mum?'

'Not exactly. I'm interning, just like you!'

Wow. Working at the same place as my girlfriend, I

thought. *Maybe we can sneak off and snog in the supply cupboard.*

'Except after today, I won't be here. I'll be at the other site in Ealing,' she said.

Bad luck, Romeo, said Hank. *Looks like the only person you'll be touching over the Xerox is yourself.*

'Oh,' I said. 'Well, this is all out of the blue. What happened?'

'I was getting bored, Joe,' she said. 'I need to stop myself drifting, you know? So my mum got me an internship working in the Marcy Slick department.'

'Marcy Slick?' I said. 'As in the goat lady?'

Mila shushed me and whispered, 'We don't mention the goat. I'll see you later.'

Then she gave me a kiss and disappeared down the corridor.

I didn't have time to think about what this would mean for our relationship, because Jackson stuck his head around his office door and barked, 'Joe, I need caffeine, stat.'

Wednesday 19th February

When I got home from work last night, I found a letter on the kitchen table. I didn't read the whole thing, but basically, the woman who lives across the corridor is a top lawyer and if Dad calls her 'Mama Cita' and tries to get her in his hot tub one more time, she will file a restraining order.

« Older posts

God, he's going to get us kicked out of the flat. I couldn't even talk to him about it, because he was out, apparently checking out a beatbox tournament and seeing if his skills were mad enough to take part.

When I arrived at work this morning, Jackson was already waiting for me.

'Exciting day ahead, my dear boy,' he said, leading me down a different corridor to the usual one.

'Um, OK,' I said. 'So what are we up to?'

'We?' he said. 'Today, there is no we. I'm having a pow-wow with a new boyband I'm trying to sign, and you are moving to an exciting new role.'

What, is he letting him loose on tea now? said Hank.

'PGS has come in for some flak recently. People are saying the product we're putting out isn't fresh and exciting enough. So I've decided to involve you in the process. You're young, hip, and happening.'

One out of three ain't bad, said Hank.

'So I know you'll be good at it. All you have to do is listen to the demos that artists send in and pass the best ones on to me.'

Oh God. How am I going to do this? I don't know any-thing about new music. My favourite band is Pink *cock-ing* Floyd!

'That seems like a lot of responsibility,' I said.

We stopped outside a room. 'You won't be alone,' said

Jackson. 'I'm teaming you up with another young buck.'

He went to open the door, then stopped. 'I should warn you,' he said, 'Horatio is the PGS President's son. He's a nice enough guy, but he's a little . . . stunted.'

'Stunted?' I said. 'What do you mean?'

Jackson opened the door to a poky little room. Inside, a tall man in a suit way more expensive-looking than mine was holding a pocket mirror really close to his face.

'Good morning, fellows,' he said. 'Don't mind me, just checking for any stray nasal hairs.'

Jackson raised his eyebrows at me and said, 'I'll leave you guys to it,' before walking away really fast.

Horatio put down the mirror and looked at me. He's about twenty-one and perfectly normal-looking except for the fact that he seems to have about fifty square metres of teeth in his gob. Honestly, they're like two rows of white tombstones.

'Yah, the name's Horatio.'

'Hi, I'm J—'

'Ghastly business,' he said. 'I'm supposed to be a junior executive for Daddy's company and they send me down here to listen to these godawful things.' He nodded at a pile of CDs. 'I'd wager the old man still hasn't forgiven me for crashing his Merc into a swimming pool. I said, "Bloody hell, Pater. You've got six more where that came from." At any rate, I'm awfully sorry about this, but I must dash. My old chum Boris is opening a new restaurant and I've agreed to have a spot of breakfast there. Knowing that scoundrel, it might end up being an all-dayer, though. Toodle-pip!'

And with that, he was gone. I began to question whether that really happened, but I noticed he left his nose hair clippers on the table which I took as definite proof of his existence.

Of course, him sodding off for a Boris breakfast meant I had more work to do, but really, how hard could listening to some CDs be?

Turns out surprisingly hard. I mean, I like to think I have a long attention span. Just the other night, I sat through Harry's running commentary/historical inaccuracies critique of Saving Private Ryan and only fell asleep twice. But this CD thing was testing that to breaking point.

I found myself drifting off, only to find that the CD had finished and I couldn't remember a thing about it.

At about four, I took the six CDs I picked out from the pile of a hundred into Jackson's office. Within fifteen minutes, he called me back.

He was leaning on his desk, propping his head on his hand. *This is it*, I thought, *I've discovered the next Beatles on my first go and he's calling me in to tell me he's resigning and giving me his job and the keys to his yacht.*

'This music, Joe,' he said.

Here it comes . . .

'Is the worst pile of crap I've heard in my life.'

Oh.

'What do you mean?'

'What do I mean?' Jackson picked them up and dropped them into his wastepaper basket one by one. 'I mean they're terrible. They all sound like Pink Floyd.'

This is an amber alert, said Norman. *Someone has disrespected the* Floyd. *Launch defensive speech.*

Which one? asked another control room worker in a hard hat. *'Best British band of all time', or 'you wouldn't get it—you're not an intellectual'?*

Neither! Hank snapped. *He's trying to convince this guy he's hip, not hip replacement.*

'I thought maybe that sound was due a comeback.'

'Good God,' he said. 'It looks like I'm going to have to send you out into the world to find out what's happening on the scene. Where's Horatio?'

I didn't know what to do. Are you supposed to cover for

« Older posts

your work colleagues? I remember lying for Ad at school when he didn't turn up to lessons because he was in town trying to buy ninja stars from Scabby Barry. Maybe I was expected to do the same thing here.

'He, um, had a . . .' I stopped and thought about his mutant mega choppers. 'Dentist's appointment.'

Not bad. That could potentially explain why he was gone so long. I mean, imagine trying to put a filling in one of those things. You'd need a cement lorry.

Jackson nodded. 'Well, starting from tomorrow, I need the two of you working harder than ever. Take the day off and get here for five. Then you can have a couple of hours of demo listening before you hit the clubs. Let's see if you can become my dream team, eh?'

Before I could say anything, the door behind me opened and Horatio stuck his head in.

'Sorry, chaps,' he said. 'Had to dash for a . . .' He stopped and winked at me with all the subtlety of a cricket bat to the face. 'Doctor's appointment.'

Dream team? Yeah right.

Friday 21st February

FROM: Joe Cowley
TO: Natalie Tuft
Subject: A&R

Hi Natalie,

Thank you for your email dated Thursday 20th February. I henceforth enclose my considered reply.

I have been in A & R since Monday and still have no knob-kicking idea what I'm doing. I've been paired up with the poshest/stupidest man in the universe. You ever seen that old horror film *The Fly*? Well imagine Ad got in the transporter pod with a minor Royal and that's what Horatio is like.

So last night, the two of us were sent out on the town to watch a load of live bands and report back to Jackson with the best ones.

Now, you know how I don't know that much about music? Well, compared to Horatio, I'm basically a genius. When I asked him if he'd ever seen live music before, he said, 'We might have had the London Phil-

« Older posts

harmonic at one of our garden parties once, but I was too bloody blotto to be certain, I'm afraid.'

So it was pretty much down to me to try to spot a future star. I couldn't help thinking how great it would have been if you were with me.

Cos you really like music. That's all. I mean, remember when Harry and Ad played us their demo and I thought it was a load of cack, but you were amazed? I don't know, I guess you're really good at seeing the potential in things.

We started at this bar in Soho. It was the first one on the itinerary Jackson had given me. It was freezing outside, and I was just grateful for a chance to get warm. Inside, there was a bloke playing beats on a laptop while another bloke with a belly-button-length beard rapped about breakfast cereal. I mean, it was different, but I didn't think they were the massive money-makers Jackson was looking for. Horatio agreed, describing it as a 'dreadful din', so we decided to get out of there and head to the next venue.

This place was very different. Sweat ran down the walls, the floors were sticky and it was rammed with long-haired people headbutting each other to what sounded like a bear firing an Uzi. Horatio stood by the door with his hands clamped over his ears. I found out the band were called Satan's Scrote. Definitely not the next big thing. I got out of there when a strand of this bloke's greasy hair landed in my lemonade.

The third venue was where it got interesting. The band were just walking out on stage, but already, I was impressed. They LOOKED different, especially the lead singer. He wasn't your typical rock-band front-man. He was rail thin, with hair that stood on top of his head in massive spikes and a crazy look in his eyes.

I prayed that the music would be as exciting as their look, and I was not disappointed. From beginning to end, I was transfixed. The singer twirled around the stage playing super-fast guitar solos and singing notes so high, only dogs could hear them.

I loved their lyrics, too. They were about aliens and robots and shady government conspiracies. They were basically taking the coolest things in the world and setting them to kick-ass rock music.

I knew I was watching the birth of something great.

« Older posts

I mean, the crowd already knew every word to every song.

Horatio wasn't keen though, and left halfway through their set, saying something about popping to the Ritz for a gala with Lady Gabriella de Bergenstrom. Whatever. I couldn't wait until Jackson saw them—an incredible live band with a ready-made fan base. I could see him shaking me by the hand and congratulating me on being a top-notch A & R man who just discovered one of the greatest bands ever. Then PGS would have no choice but to put me in charge of the SOUND EXPERIENCE and allow them to make whatever album they wanted.

Sadly, when I gave Jackson my written report, the reaction wasn't as great as I had hoped.

'Mews?' he spat the name out like a mouldy olive.
I was like, 'Yeah, they were amazing.'
He said, 'How the hell did you get into the music business, Joe?'
'Um, by being . . . great?'
He slammed his hand down on the desk and said, 'Mews are a tribute band. Have you never heard of M U S E—Muse?'

I shook my head and was like, 'No. Why, are they famous?'

'Oh no,' he said. 'They're only one of the biggest rock bands in the world, but other than that, they're just a bunch of chancers.' He pinched the bridge of his nose. 'I can't believe I give you free rein of all the live music in London and you bring me a bloody tribute band. I expected this of Horatio, but not you.'

Of course, I could have told him that Horatio didn't even want to be there and sodded off to go hob-nobbing with Lady Catherine of Aragon or whatever the cocking hell her name was, but for some reason, I didn't.

'Do you want me to go out again tonight?' I said.
He said, 'No, I think you've done enough.'

Looks like it's back to making coffee for me!

Cowley
PS Have you ever heard of Muse?

FROM: Natalie Tuft
TO: Joe Cowley
Subject: RE: A&R

« Older posts

HAHAHAHAHAHAHAHAHAAAAAAAAAAAAAAAAAA!

Saturday 22nd February

Me and Mila hadn't seen each other much this week, so we decided to go out for dinner tonight.

It was just nice to get away from the flat for a few hours. Everyone was doing their own thing, sick of living in each other's pockets. Harry was in the living room watching a history documentary on the laptop with his earphones in, Greeny was in his room, probably on the phone to Scott, and Ad was having a rubber ducky race in the hot tub. I don't even want to talk about what Dad was doing, but let's just say our downstairs neighbours didn't appreciate his attempts at breakdancing.

Anyway, we ended up at this place called *La Maison,* which is super fancy, and when I saw the prices on the menu, I basically had a full-blown panic attack and wondered if it would be acceptable for me to order tap water for dinner. Luckily, Mila said she was paying.

I mean, that's fine, isn't it? The girl paying? This is the twenty-first century, isn't it? I went to the bathroom and consulted **Men's Domain** on my phone. They basically said it's cool, but if you make a habit of it, she might think you're a deadbeat. I made a mental note to look out for two-for-one restaurant coupons in the newspaper.

The food there was really nice, even if I wasn't sure what any of it was, what with it all being in French. I mean, it was stuff like 'vin rouge' and 'entrée' and 'soup du jour'. What the hell did any of those things mean? Not that I let on to Mila. She speaks French fluently. And English. And Dutch. And German. And Spanish. And I remember a time when I felt clever for knowing a few phrases in Klingon.

'So,' I said, after she'd finished a full-blown Frenchy conversation with the waitress. 'How was your first week at work?'

Mila nibbled on a piece of bread and her eyes went massive. 'Oh my God, Joe, SO good. I'm assisting the people who are organizing Marcy's comeback tour.'

'Wow,' I said. 'I thought she'd retired for good.'

Mila shook her head. 'No. She's about to announce a surprise tour. Like a week before the actual dates. It's going to be a huge surprise so *shhh*. I'm only making coffee and filing, but it's nice to be part of something so cool. Anyway, enough about me, tell me what you've been up to.'

Well, I did. And I think I might have given off the impression that I'm not having as much fun as she is. It might have been how I told her about how terrible I am at it. It might have been how I spent ten minutes calling Horatio a 'massive weird giraffe-looking deserter'. It might have been how I begged her to put a word in for me with her mum so I can work with her.

« Older posts

'Oh, I don't know about that,' she said, sipping some of her wine, which made my glass of Diet Coke look kind of pathetic. 'I think they have enough people.'

I sighed. 'But your mum is an executive—surely she can sort something out.'

Mila shook her head and said, 'I'm sorry, Joe,' in a way that said 'case closed'.

Before I could question why she was so against us working together, a voice from behind interrupted.

'Of all the eating joints in all the Smizzoke, I had to walk into the same one as my main man, the J-Dawg!'

No. NO. NOOOOOO!

I turned around, and there was Dad, decked out in a bright purple suit and medallion with a blonde woman who had to be about the same age as Svetlana.

'Hey, shawty,' he said to the waitress. 'Is it cool if we pull our tables together? We be having a double date up in this bizzitch!'

Mila watched open-mouthed as Dad dragged another table next to ours and sat next to her.

'Irina, this is my boy, Joe, and his chica, Mila. Guys, this is my date, Irina.'

Irina? said Hank. *Say what you like about the guy—he has a type.*

Irina, who looked like she would rather be anywhere else in the world than at that table, muttered a 'Hello.'

'So what are the odds of us ending up in the same joint, at the same time, with our respective fly girls?' said Dad.

'I am not your fly girl,' said Irina.

'It is amazing,' I said. 'It's almost as if you overheard me telling Greeny where I was going and made your own reservations.'

Dad laughed and did that Jamaican finger-clicky thing he does. 'Hey, if that's how it is, maybe I just wanted to spend a bit more time with my boy, see if he could talk me up to my date.'

I looked at Irina and guessed that even if I told her Dad had a knob that peed pound coins, she wouldn't be impressed.

'Keith has really done wonders with the flat,' said Mila. I know her well enough to spot her 'trying to be nice' voice.

It's the same one she does when faking an interest in Harry's pipe collection.

'True dat,' said Dad. 'I've totally pimped it. You know what I mean by pimped, don't you, Irina?'

Irina looked at the table and said, 'Back in Vladivostok, a pimp shot my grandmother.'

Dad glanced at me, then at Mila. 'Who's up for drinks?' he said.

What followed was the most awkward meal of my life. No one knew what to say. I kept reading the wine list, just so I had something to do with my hands.

'So, Irina,' said Dad as the waitress cleared our plates, 'I've started freestyling recently. Want to hear a verse?'

'I have to go to the bathroom,' she said, and got up.

Dad chuckled to himself. 'I'm sure she'll be back soon.'

As we watched her walk straight past the bathroom and out of the door, he stopped chuckling.

'It's OK,' said Mila, doing her nice voice again, 'there are plenty more fish in the barrel.'

Some of her English phrases are a bit off.

'I don't get it,' said Dad. 'She saw my dating profile, so she knew what I was about.'

Mila's eyes flitted over to me briefly. 'Would you mind if I had a look? Sometimes a woman's eye can help.'

Dad passed his phone over to Mila. I watched her face change from concealed amusement, to concern, to 'how the hell am I going to find the words for this?'

'Um, Keith,' she said, 'how old is this photo?'

Dad shrugged. 'Couple of years.'

I leaned over to get a closer look. 'That pram in the background. I'm in it, aren't I?'

Dad gulped then looked around the room. 'Yo, we're going to need the bill over here!'

I asked Mila if she wanted to hang out at the flat for a while after dinner, but she didn't seem keen for some reason. Probably because she's realized there's a chance I'll end up like Dad and she doesn't want anything more to do with me. Can't blame her, to be honest. I've already told Harry that if he ever catches me saying 'wicked fresh', he has my permission to take me into a field and shoot me.

Monday 24th February

I had it all planned out. I was going to leave the office at 1 p.m., buy a bouquet of flowers, get on the District Line at 1.10 p.m. and be at Mila's office in Ealing by 1.29 p.m. That would give me seven minutes with her before I had to get the Tube back to work.

« Older posts

I suppose I wanted to remind her that despite who my dad is, I'm a normal person.

Anyway, that's all irrelevant because I didn't get the chance to see her. As soon as I got in, Jackson called me and Horatio into his office.

I thought this was it. I thought I was getting sacked and would be back home in Tammerstone within hours. No more Mila. No more chance to reinvent myself as a cool guy. I'd probably end up as one of those scallies that buzz around the estate on tiny motorbikes, getting chased by PCSOs.

'Right, lads,' said Jackson. 'The reason I'm calling you in is there's been a change of plan.'

Here we go, said Hank. *Better start packing.*

'Due to a staffing emergency, I'm going to have to ask you to change duties.'

Oh.

Jackson leaned towards us. 'You're going to be acting as personal assistants to Niles Perkins.'

Norman tapped something into a computer console. *Niles Perkins—member of multi-platinum-selling boy band, FTW. He has been voted World's Dreamiest Heart-throb four years in a row.*

Wait a sec, said Hank. *Why does Joe have all this in his brain?*

'Pardon me, McHugh,' said Horatio. 'But is there no one

else who can do it? I have a pressing engagement at the Ivy this arvo.'

'It'll have to wait,' said Jackson. 'The PA he usually has just quit, so I have no choice. I have faith that the two of you will do a good job. I know you have experience of looking after celebrity guests at your dad's hotel in Mayfair, Horatio.'

Horatio just huffed and folded his arms.

Jackson pulled a file out of his desk and slid it over to us. 'All your info is in there. Niles is going to be in London until Friday night, and you have to be on hand to meet his every need.'

I picked up the file. *Every need? I hope he knows how to wipe his own bum.*

'Is he going to be on his own?' I asked. 'I heard rumours he was going solo.'

Again, kid, said Hank, *why do you know so much about this particular boy band?*

'Don't believe the hype,' said Jackson. 'Oh, that reminds me.' He passed us a sheet of paper. 'I'm going to need you both to sign this.'

I looked at it. On the top it read 'Non-disclosure Agreement'.

I glanced at Horatio to see what he thought, but he was still sulking.

'It's just a formality,' Jackson said. 'It's to say you agree that you will not breathe a word of what you see in the FTW camp to anyone, not even your mother.'

I hesitated. The last time Jackson gave me a contract, I ended up regretting it.

'What if . . . I don't want to?' I said.

'Then I'll sack you for refusing to do your job.'

I signed it.

We arrived at Heathrow an hour later in a limo. A proper limo—not like that abomination Dad got us. I decided to sit in the front, because Horatio was annoying me with his moaning. I regretted that decision when I met the driver and his chronic fart problem though.

We had to push our way through throngs of screaming girls at the arrivals gate, all holding 'I HEART FTW' placards.

Once we'd got to a clearing, I turned to Horatio, lolloping towards me like a sedated, aristocratic emu.

'Listen,' I said. 'I am way out of my depth here, so I can't have you disappearing again. I don't care if the Count of Bumshire is throwing a masquerade ball.'

Horatio grumbled under his breath and started picking at the crest on his blazer.

I quickly found the designated assistants' area. There were four others there. Before I could introduce us, an unearthly scream ripped through the air and nearly burst my eardrums. It was FTW coming up the ramp.

They started to appear in our little enclosure, each flanked by two huge minders. First Lance, then Harvey, then Seamus, then Min-Soo. It was mad, really. These huge megastars I had seen on TV, on billboards . . .

And on your bedroom wall, apparently, said Hank.

. . . were right in front of me. I was star-struck. Then, as quickly as they arrived, they were gone again, paired up with their assistants.

Some of the crowd followed the rest of the band, but most of them stayed. Everyone knows that Niles is the favourite and they were desperate to catch a glimpse of him. When the papers reported that he was dating the American singer Maria Sanchez, the record company had to set up a helpline with trained counsellors.

Dozens of people filed in, but there was no sign of Niles. I started to panic. Had we missed him? Was he going to attempt to wander the streets of London, and end up getting crushed under an avalanche of hormones and selfie sticks?

I turned to Horatio for support but he was on the phone to someone called Tarquin, talking about how lazy his pool boy is. I peered down the ramp. The flight crew were walking up. We really had missed him!

That's it—I'm done! I thought. *I'll be back in crappy Tammerstone by the end of the day, lying in my old bunk bed, listening to Gav farting and scratching his nugs.*

They were a weird-looking flight crew, though. The pilot was openly flirting with the air hostesses. In fact, he had his arms around them. And do pilots wear jeans? Maybe this was a really relaxed airline.

It was only when they got close that I realized who it was.

'*Ohh, Niles,* you are *terrible,*' the air hostess said.

'I know, baby,' he said. 'Born that way.'

Oh, thank sweet baby Jesus in his manger.

'Niles!' I called after him.

He ignored me and asked the air hostesses if they wanted to 'get out of here'.

He was about to walk straight out into the maelstrom, but I grabbed his arm and stopped him.

'Oh, hey, man,' he said when he saw me. 'You my assistant?'

'Um, yes.'

He examined my face, as if he was trying to figure out if I was a replicant or something like that. 'Where's Tiffany?'

'She's . . . unavailable,' I said. 'I'm Joe, and this is Horatio.'

I stuck my hand out for a shake, but Niles just tipped his pilot hat and said, 'Lead on, bro.'

We got out to the limo, after nearly being dismembered by the mob. 'Are your security on the way?' I yelled over the deafening screaming.

'Nah, man, that's not how I roll any more,' he said. 'I want no barrier between me and my fans.'

'NILES, CAN I HAVE A SELFIE WITH YOU?' a girl screamed right down my ear.

'No, you may not,' he replied, and jumped into the back of the limo. Horatio got in with him.

I got in the front, and we pulled away, narrowly avoiding crushing half of the UK's Tumblr users.

As we went through the barrier, I saw identical limos ahead of us.

'So how come they don't travel together?' I asked the farty driver.

He laughed and shook his head. 'You've got a lot to learn, kid.'

According to the itinerary Jackson gave me, the first stop was the *Kevin Strawberry Show*, which is filmed at some studios on the other side of London. We had an hour to get there and, if traffic wasn't too bad, we should arrive on time.

We had been on the road for about ten minutes when the divider came down and Niles appeared behind us.

'Stop the limo!' he said.

I turned around and tried to look all calming and reassuring, but probably had a face like a stressed weasel. 'What's the matter, Niles?' I asked.

'I want him out,' he said, pointing at Horatio.

I glared at him. What the hell had he done?

'Why's that?'

'Because I remember who he is now,' he said. 'At our last album launch, he tried it on with my girlfriend and did nasty stuff to one of the ice sculptures.'

I gave Horatio the stink-eye.

'While I have no recollection of that, I must admit it does seem rather likely,' he said.

'Stop the limo. Now,' Niles said.

The driver pulled into a layby and Niles leaned over and opened the door. 'Out.'

'Here?' Horatio cried. 'But we're right next to a housing estate. And there's a Toby Carvery over there. It's ghastly!'

'Don't care,' said Niles. 'You're out.'

I tried to reason with him, but he wouldn't listen and I got the impression that what Niles says goes. Horatio got out of the car and we pulled away, leaving him standing next to an overflowing bin, looking like a giraffe who'd just wandered into a lion's den.

When we pulled away, I started freaking out. How the hell was I supposed to look after a world famous pop star by myself?

Calm down, Joe, said Norman. *Think of this as an opportunity. If you can do this, you'll be sure to get a promotion.*

Yeah, and you won't have to share the glory with that Horatio moron, either, said Hank.

That was a good point. This was exactly the thing I needed to get back in Jackson's good books after the whole Mews fiasco. I was going to personally assist this Niles better than any personal assistant had ever personally assisted him before.

The partition came down again.

'Hello, lads,' said Niles, his voice all hushed. 'I hate to be that guy, but I need a wee.'

I exchanged a look with the driver.

'There's a service station a couple of miles up the road,' said the driver. 'We can stop there.'

'Wicked,' said Niles. 'I'll be super quick, promise.'

The driver and me stood next to a Minion grabber machine outside the toilets. My eye started twitching like crazy.

'He's been twenty minutes in there,' I said. 'What could he be doing?'

The driver shrugged. 'In my experience, everything and anything. I used to drive Min-Soo, but I fell out with my boss and he gave me Niles as punishment.'

I checked my watch again. 'We're going to be late for the show,' I said.

The driver nodded and thumbed through a nudey mag

he'd bought from the shop. 'Yep.'

I huffed. 'Well, thanks for all your help.'

'You're welcome,' he said, raising an eyebrow at the centrefold.

I couldn't take any more so I marched into the toilets to find Niles. When I got in there, they were empty. I checked every cubicle. Nothing. That was when I noticed the open window. Oh no.

I turned and ran outside. Niles was wearing the captain's hat and shades, so he was slightly disguised, but that would only get him so far. I frantically scanned the horizon for him, but he was nowhere to be seen.

No! How could I lose him? My phone buzzed in my pocket. Text from Jackson.

My ppl tell me Niles isn't at studio. WHAT IS HAPPENING?

I felt tears brimming in my eyes. What a nightmare. I decided to scour the perimeter of the car park for him. Hopefully, he hadn't got far.

I heard weird music coming from around the corner. When I got there, I found Niles sitting on one of those little kid's rides. When it stopped, he put another fifty-pence coin in and it started again.

'Are you OK, Niles?'

He said nothing.

'We should probably get going.'

« Older posts

Still nothing.

'You'll be late for the show.'

'I'm not going,' he said. 'This is my happy place. I'm staying here.'

'Y-your happy place?'

He nodded. 'This was my favourite TV show as a kid.'

I clasped my hands together to stop them shaking. 'So you're not doing the show?'

Niles shook his head. 'That going to be a problem?'

'Well, kind of,' I said. 'I mean, if you don't, I'll probably get sacked.'

The ride stopped and he cocked an eyebrow at me. 'That right?'

'Yes.'

He sighed. 'Well, I guess I'd better come quietly, then.'

'Thank you, Niles, I really app—'

'Right after this,' he said, before dropping a two-pound coin into the slot.

After fielding ten angry phone calls from Jackson and nearly having an actual real cardiac arrest, we arrived at the studio forty-five minutes late.

Apparently, they couldn't wait any longer and had to go ahead and do the interview without Niles. He wasn't having it, though, and ran out onto the set and sat on Harvey's lap. Then afterwards he made us drive around London, blasting kids' TV themes out of the window.

Maybe making coffee wasn't so bad.

Tuesday 25th February

Happy birthday to me.

I dragged myself out of bed, exhausted. Turns out looking after insane boy-banders takes it out of you.

I got a FaceTime from home—Mum, Jim, Holly, Ivy, Gav, and Poppy were there.

'Hello, Oh!' the twins yelled. They haven't got the hang of J's yet. Ivy grabbed the iPad and kissed the screen, which meant Mum had to disappear into the kitchen for a cloth to wipe off what must have been one hell of a chocolatey smear.

'How are you, my boy?' she asked when she got back. 'Are you eating well? Are you staying out of trouble? Have you been to see the Queen? How's the band going?'

Well, I attempted to answer all of those questions, but I was mostly trying to hide the fact that I was kind of choked.

« Older posts

Seeing them all again made me realize how much I miss them. Holly and Ivy have changed loads in the time I've been away—they're becoming like proper little people.

Straight afterwards, I bought myself a train ticket to go home this weekend. I thought it would be nice to surprise them. I decided to book one for Mila, too. She always said she wanted to visit Tammerstone again. I have no idea why.

I was about to head to PGS to meet the limo, when Harry, Ad, and Greeny emerged from their rooms.

'Ah, Joe, glad we could catch you in time,' said Harry. 'We'd hate for you to think we'd forgotten your seventeenth birthday, old bean.'

'Oh,' I said. 'Thanks.'

'That's all right, mate,' said Ad. 'Trouble is, cos we've been recording this stupid album, we haven't had much time to go out and buy you a present.'

'So we got Greeny to make you one,' said Harry. 'Show him, Greeny.'

Greeny grinned and pulled an A3-sized poster from behind his back. On it was FTW, posing in just their underpants. Then I noticed he'd Photoshopped my face onto Seamus's. What makes it worse is that he has his arm around Niles.

'Yeah, thanks,' I said, as the three of them collapsed in hysterics.

Great. The only thing that cheers them up is humiliating

me. Some things never change.

To make things worse, Dad then decided to join us.

'Yo, yo, yo, my b'day b-boy, how's it hanging?' he said. 'Here, I got you a little sumpin' sumpin'.'

He handed me a small box. What could it be? A thousand quid? A legally binding note saying he is moving out today?

I opened the box.

'Oh,' I said. 'This is . . . nice.'

I lifted out the most enormous gold necklace I'd ever seen in my life.

'Good Lord,' said Harry. 'I never thought I would be friends with the Lord Mayor of London.'

'What are you waiting for?' said Dad. 'Try it on.'

I did as I was told. It almost dragged me to the ground.

'Lads,' said Dad, draping his arms over their shoulders, 'I can't begin to tell you how proud I am of my boy. Watching him become a man, getting a job, and a hot chica—it's a privilege, but it goes by too fast. I can't believe it's seventeen years since his mum was lying on her back, groaning and panting. But enough about the night he was conceived.'

Oh GODDDDDDDD.

Harry and Greeny fell about laughing and Ad muttered something about Dad being the luckiest man ever.

« Older posts

'So I say we celebrate,' Dad went on. 'How about we all head to the casino tonight? I'll teach you to shoot craps.'

Harry sniggered. 'Tempting as that sounds, old son, we're recording late tonight.'

'And I'm out with Mila,' I said. 'Just me and her. No double-dating.'

'Oh,' said Dad. 'That's all right, y'all. Now, Joe, remember to sling that bling for me!'

I agreed, then waited until he went back to his room before chucking it in my bottom drawer with a loud clank.

Anyway, after an epic bollocking from Jackson about letting Niles be late for Kevin Strawberry, me and the driver set off to pick Niles up from his hotel. He had a photoshoot first thing, followed by an afternoon of interviews.

I got the concierge to give Niles's room a call. No answer. I waited ten minutes then got him to try again. Nothing. In the end, I went up there and knocked. After about five minutes, he emerged. His hair was all over the place, and I'm sure his arm had one more tattoo than it did yesterday.

'Heyyy, Joe,' he drawled. 'What are you doing here? It's the middle of the night!'

'No it isn't,' I said. 'It's half nine in the morning and you have twenty minutes to get to a photoshoot.'

Niles blinked heavily and said, 'Well, how about that? All right, man, come on in. I'll be two secs.'

I couldn't believe the size of the room. Whenever I've stayed in hotels, there isn't enough room to swing a cat. In this one, you could swing a tiger. It was so huge, I almost didn't notice that the carpet was made of humans.

Well, there were a lot of people lying around. Some of them clothed, some not. It looked like some kind of massacre.

''Scuse the mess,' said Niles. 'Had a bit of a get-together.'

A get-together?! The only get-together I've ever been to was at my nan and granddad's house and the most exciting thing that happened there was Uncle Johnny having too many snowballs and tripping over the bird bath.

'This is a, um, nice hotel room,' I said, desperately trying to think of something to fill the silence.

Niles smiled thinly. 'If I had all the money I was entitled to, I could buy this entire hotel.'

Before I could ask what that meant, Niles threw on the same T-shirt he was wearing yesterday, ran a hand through his hair and headed out.

When we got down to the car, I was about to get in the front, but Niles stopped me.

'Nah, you can ride in the back today, bro,' he said. 'Gets boring with no one to talk to.'

I nodded, but inside I was freaking out. What was I going to talk about with one of the most famous people in the world? **STAR TREK**? I bet he couldn't even name the commander of the Enterprise-D, which is totally basic stuff.

Niles pulled down his shades and sprawled across the leather seat. I sat on the other side and fastened my seat belt.

'So what's new with you?' he said.

What *was* new with me? I suppose I was worried that I wasn't cool enough for my girlfriend, and that I wasn't good enough to be doing this job, and that really I belonged back in Tammerstone, hanging out with Mad Morris and dipping bins for fag ends.

'Um, it's my birthday today.'

Niles lifted his shades and cocked an eyebrow at me. 'Seriously?'

I nodded.

'Many happy returns, my man,' he said. 'How old are you?'

I cleared my throat. 'Seventeen.'

He reached into the on-board fridge and pulled out a can of Red Bull. 'Wicked. I remember my seventeenth birthday. We'd just had our first number one record. They were good times.'

He was smiling, but then it faded and he looked really sad. 'The best times.'

It went proper awkward, then.

Now look, kid, said Hank. *I know your first instinct in these situations is to start talking, but we both know that's a bad idea. Just keep it zipped.*

Oh, I don't know about that, said Norman. *I think Joe has somewhat developed as a conversationalist these past few months. I think he'll be fine without our guidance.*

'So, it looked like it was a fun party last night,' I said. 'Fun parties are . . . fun.'

You were saying? said Hank.

'Was OK,' said Niles. 'Once you've been around the block a couple of times, they all start to blur into one.'

'I hope Maria doesn't mind!'

I winced as soon as I'd said it. I kind of felt as if a mere pleb like me shouldn't have been talking about celebrities.

Niles took a deep swig from his can and leaned towards me. 'Listen, bro,' he said. 'You've signed that thing that stops you blabbing, right?'

I nodded.

'Good,' he said. 'Cos here's the thing. Me and Maria aren't a real couple.'

Holy crap! Hank yelled. *Is there any way you can destroy that form? The papers would pay top dollar for this!*

'What do you mean?'

'It's a sham,' he said. 'Her last single tanked, so I did her a favour. To keep her in the public eye.'

'Oh,' I said. 'That's kind of—'

'Sad?' Niles cut in. 'Depressing? Makes you feel all dirty?'

'Um . . . yes.'

'Tell me about it,' he said. 'But I've got a feeling it's run its course.'

He pulled out his phone and said, 'Ah ha! This one got out in record time.'

He tossed the phone over to me.

CelebGoss.com

Niles Perkins cheats on Maria with five Page 3 models.

Hotel guests tell of debauched party.

WATCH EXCLUSIVE VID HERE!!!

I rubbed my forehead. 'Was this a planned thing?'

Niles laughed as he crushed his empty can and bounced it off the ceiling.

'Nope. I've been getting sick of these suits telling me what to do. I just want to be me, you know? Show the world my true personality.'

Yeah, a freakin' wackadoodle, said Hank.

When we got to the studio, the rest of the band were waiting and started a sarcastic slow clap. Niles didn't care. He climbed onto a clothes chest and clapped.

'Attention, please,' he yelled. 'Today is my man Joe's birthday, and I am not going to begin this shoot until we have all sung to him.'

Everyone groaned while I went as red as a London bus

with high blood pressure.

'Oh, pack it in, Niles,' Harvey droned.

'I mean it,' said Niles. 'On three, we're all going to sing. Even the FTW lads, and I know you hate to do that without a backing track.' He winked at them as they glared like they wanted to forcibly remove his spleen.

'I'm not singing to him,' said Min-Soo. 'Who is he, anyway?'

This bloke who must have been the photographer wiped sweat from his forehead, and said, 'Please, just sing so we can get on with it. I don't have all day.'

The photographer must have been a big deal, because they all obeyed him and serenaded me with the most half-hearted rendition of 'Happy Birthday' you've ever heard in your life.

I mean, yes, it was embarrassing, but I was living the dream of millions of girls all over the world.

I'd like to say that Niles calmed down after that, but he didn't. He kept mooning at the camera, and during the radio interviews he would only speak in a made-up language called Kokobashi.

'The lads used to love that,' he said, in the limo back to the hotel. 'Back when we were at school, I'd talk Kokobashi to the teachers all the time. This once, Lance laughed so much he weed himself. These days, they think they're too good for it. Everything is so serious. I hate it.'

« Older posts

'I did wonder why you were all in separate limos,' I said.

Niles nodded. 'It never used to be that way. This business though, it changes people. Wrecks friendships.'

When I got back to the flat, Harry, Ad, and Greeny were trying to take their minds off the stress of the album by buckarooing Dad. He'd fallen asleep in front of *Hip-Hop Classix* and they'd managed to get three pillows, a kettle, a toaster, and next door's Bichon Frise on him before he woke up. It was proper funny.

There's no way we'll go the same way as FTW.

There's just no way.

Wednesday 26th February

What a cocking day.

Mila took me out for my birthday last night. She tried to order us a bottle of wine, but the barman wanted to see my ID, so I had to drink Diet Coke instead. And he got dead huffy when I asked him to serve it in a wine glass.

To be honest, I'm not that bothered. I sneakily drank some wine at my nan's 'get-together' and it tasted horrible. I looked at the label and, apparently, it was made in 1982! No wonder it tasted so rank! I tipped the rest down the sink before anyone else could be poisoned.

Mila bought me a watch as a present and talked about how excited she is about her job. She was saying they're now letting her sit in on auditions for Marcy's backing band and even sometimes ask her opinion.

Maybe when the two of us are established, we can team up and start our own music organization.

When I got back in from dinner, Dad was still up, sitting in the hot tub, obviously refreshed from his nap/burial.

'I forgot to tell you, J-Dawg,' he said. 'You had a parcel today. I think the guys balanced it on my face. I put it on the kitchen counter.'

Weird. I hadn't ordered anything. I went over and opened it. There was a little birthday card inside. It had a picture of a frog in a party hat on the front. When I opened it up, my stomach did a little flip.

« Older posts

Happy bday Cowley,

How does it feel to be OLD?!

Yours geriatrically,

Nat x

PS Soz for the crap card. Discount Party Zone doesn't have the best selection!

Then I lifted out the gift.

I'm not sure how long I'd been staring at it when Dad said, 'Hey, how come you're not wearing the chain?'

'So what's the plan for today?' Niles asked when he finally answered the door.

He had massive bags under his eyes and looked proper fed up. I knew how he felt. I'd just got off the phone with Jackson.

'ARE YOU TRYING TO AGGRAVATE MY STOMACH ULCERS, JOE? I'VE BEEN FIELDING CALLS FROM THE PRESS ALL NIGHT ABOUT NILES'S ERRATIC BEHAVIOUR. WHAT'S HORATIO DOING?'

I don't know why I didn't throw him under the bus. I guess I was still holding onto the hope that I could do it all myself. If Jackson found out Horatio had gone, he might have forced him to come back and ruined everything.

'You're shooting a video for your next single,' I said to Niles.

I was slightly relieved that he didn't have to be there until midday. I'd told him it was ten, though. It meant we had a chance of being on time.

He was wearing a beanie hat that he must have piled all his hair into. It looked proper weird.

'So,' I said to Niles once we set off. 'Is everything going to be all right today? No dramas? No mooning at cameras? No Kokobashi?'

Niles looked at me with his sad cow eyes and sighed. 'Nah, everything's going to be cool.'

Then he turned to the window and whipped his beanie off.

Holy mother of Buddha, said Hank.

Now, you must remember to stay calm, Joe, said Norman. *But it might be an idea to ask what happened to his, um . . . head.*

'Niles?'

He looked at me again. 'What's up?'

'Your, um, hair.'

'Yeah?'

'Well, I couldn't help but notice . . . I don't know if you're aware . . . your hair is . . . gone.'

He was completely bald. Not just bald like I was when Roger the barber gave me a number one all over, I mean COMPLETELY bald. Like balder than Picard. His scalp was as smooth as a hard-boiled egg.

'Oh that?' said Niles as if it was nothing. 'It's cool. Just part of my evolution.'

I cleared my throat. 'And what do you mean by that, exactly?'

'Ever googled yourself, Joe?' he said.

'No.'

'Don't do it,' he said. 'It's the worst. It tells you exactly what everyone thinks about you. Like, when you type my name in, a load of suggested searches come up—Niles Perkins Maria Sanchez, Niles Perkins FTW, Niles Perkins hair.'

I nodded as if I had any idea what he was flapping his gums about.

'Hair,' he said again. 'That's all people see when they look at me.'

Not any more you freakin' fruit loop, said Hank.

'So I've taken that away from them,' he said. 'Maybe now they'll actually want to know what kind of person I am, rather than what styling products I use.'

Oh God.

'Also, Niles,' I said, 'I can't help but notice you have some . . . writing. On your scalp.'

'Oh yeah,' he said, and looked at the floor, so I could read it.

'Oh, that's nice,' I said. 'What's that, the name of your new song?'

Niles laughed bitterly and said, 'No, man. It's what I am. I'm trapped in the machine.'

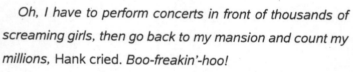 *Oh, I have to perform concerts in front of thousands of screaming girls, then go back to my mansion and count my millions,* Hank cried. *Boo-freakin'-hoo!*

'OK,' I said, wondering if I was still in bed and this was just a weird dream. 'And, just out of curiosity, does that come off?'

'Not easily,' said Niles. 'It's permanent marker.'

I felt myself beginning to hyperventilate when the limo stopped and the partition lowered.

'Here we are,' said the driver through air thick with fart fumes. 'Chedderton Studios.'

Oh crap! Sir Crapinald Crappington of Crap Hall in Crap-

« Older posts

shire! The Third! CRAP! There is no time to put this right!

Before I could stop him or suggest that the stinky-arsed driver take us for a trip round the block, or seven, Niles was out of the car, straight into the glare of the paparazzi.

CRRAAAAAAAAAAAAAAAAAAAAAAAAAAAAP-PPPPPP!

I begged them to stop taking photos but they ignored me.

'Niles, what happened to your hair?'

'Why have you drawn on your head?'

Niles didn't say anything, but just walked over to a picnic table, lifted the parasol from out of the middle and proceeded to swing it at them.

Honestly, blog, I tried to stop him, but he was like a ridiculous medieval jouster. The photographers ran away, still snapping Niles's bald, graffitied noggin. He screamed at them to stop, but they wouldn't, so he threw down the parasol, snatched a camera off the closest paparazzo and smashed it on the ground.

I was like, 'OK, that'll do,' but he didn't listen and stomped it into a million pieces, before grabbing a wodge of cash out of his back pocket and throwing it down on top.

When we got inside the studio, I struggled to keep up with Niles.

'Do you not like them, then?' I asked.

'Parasites,' he spat. 'And they're not the only ones.'

He pushed a door open that led into a make-up room. Each member of the band was being made to look even better-looking by their own artist.

'Listen up,' Niles yelled. 'I quit!'

My heart tried to smash its way out of my chest like an alien baby. I couldn't have this happen on my watch.

'Are you sure, Niles?' I murmured, but I don't think he heard me.

Lance turned around.

'First of all, you look ridiculous, and second, there's no way you're leaving. You love the fame too much.'

'SHOWS WHAT YOU KNOW!' Niles yelled, and marched back outside. I think I got a stitch trying to keep up.

When we got back to the car park, the driver was leaning against the limo, smoking. Niles plucked the cigarette from his lips and threw it away.

'Keys,' he said, his face totally blank.

'You what?' said the driver.

'Keys,' Niles said again.

'You want the keys to the limo?' the driver said. He looked at me as if to check that this was some kind of joke. All I could do was shrug.

'Hand them over.'

The driver chuckled. 'No way.'

Niles stepped closer and grabbed him by the lapels. 'I pay your wages and I say you have to give me the keys, understand?'

'Fine,' said the driver. 'Take them.'

He passed Niles the keys, and before I could do any-thing, the bald lunatic was in the driver's seat.

'Niles, no!' I called after him. 'Don't do this!'

I wrenched the passenger door open and begged him to stop.

'Listen, bro,' he said. 'I like you. But if you don't either get in or get out of my way, I'm going to have to hurt you.'

I got in.

Are you insane? Norman cried. *Get out of there right now!*

Even if I'd wanted to, I couldn't. Niles was zooming us out of the car park so fast, the G-force pinned me to my seat.

I suppose I thought I could talk him down, get him to pull over. Turns out I overestimated my powers of persuasion.

'No way, man,' he screamed as we hurtled along the country lanes at top speed. 'We're getting out of here!'

As we rounded a bend, a tractor appeared, head-ing straight towards us. Niles didn't even brake, but just swerved onto the grass verge, sending mud splattering everywhere. The tractor driver must have swerved too because loads of potatoes landed on the roof of the limo as we passed.

This can't be how we die! Norman yelled.

Norm's right, said Hank. *Imagine the newsflash. Boy-band superstar Niles Perkins has been tragically killed in a limousine wreck. Fans all over the world are in mourning. Oh and, by the way, some other jerk's dead, too.*

Niles whooped. 'Doesn't it make you feel alive, Joe?'

'No it doesn't!' I screamed. 'Quite the opposite! Can you at least slow down?'

'No chance!' he yelled. 'There is no slowing down from now on. I am the unstoppable object!'

And it was true. He didn't even stop for a red light. I clamped my hands over my eyes and screamed like a baby as a van clipped our back end and sent us spinning across the junction. We seemed to be skidding for hours.

I was violently jerked forward in my seat as we smashed into something. I seized the opportunity to jump from the car before he could attempt to drive away. When I got out, I could see that that wasn't going to happen. We were completely wrapped around a telegraph pole.

'Oi! What the bloody hell do you think you're playing at?'

I looked up and this massive bloke who I guessed must have been the van driver came stomping over.

I gulped. He did not look happy.

'You're not the driver, are you? How old are you, twelve?'

Luckily, the heat was off me as soon as the driver's door opened.

'Oh, so here's the joker that thinks red lights don't apply

to him and his stupid limo,' he said. 'Wait a minute, are you that FTW bloke?'

Soon, passers-by were filming on their phones, making sure they captured every second of Niles running around in traffic, screaming Kokobashi swear words, and finally, being arrested.

All in all, I think this assignment has gone really well.

Thursday 27th February

We got a call from Jackson last night, summoning us all to his office. I was tired as hell after spending most of the afternoon giving a statement about that maniac Niles to the police and had mentally prepared myself for the firing. For going back to Tammerstone. For watching from afar as Mila becomes the head of PGS and I become a recurring Jezza Kyle guest.

I was in the middle of practising my grovelling when my phone started ringing. I didn't recognize the number, but reasoned that it was Jackson. He was always calling from weird numbers.

'Hello?'

'Hey, Joe, how's it going?'

'Niles?' I said. 'Where are you?'

He laughed, 'Relax, bro. I'm in the joint.'

'What do you mean, the joint?'

'The big house,' he said. 'The clink. Prison. They nabbed

me for dangerous driving.'

'Well, I'm not surprised, to be honest,' I said. 'Are you going to get bail?'

'Nah,' he said. 'I'd rather stay in for a while. You know, it's not so bad in here, man. Really gives you time to think.'

This guy's insane, said Hank. *They need to ship him to the nuthouse, pronto.*

'Anyway,' Niles went on. 'I just wanted to say thanks.'

'Um, what for?'

'For sticking with me the past few days,' he said. 'It's been cool just hanging with a normal person.'

Normal? said Hank. *If only you knew, baldy.*

When I got to PGS, we were sent straight to Jackson's office. He didn't look happy. His hair seemed to be on at a weird angle.

'You had ONE job, Joe,' he said, pacing up and down. 'Do you have any idea what a disaster this is? Niles has quit the band and is in jail! We've just had a new range of Niles dolls made. How the hell are we going to sell them now?'

'You could put them in prison over-alls and shave their heads?' I said.

'SHUT UP,' Jackson barked.

I shut up.

'How can I trust you to look after XPERIENCE? I mean, what would happen? Would the stupid one end up going down for murder?'

'Nah, Greeny would never kill anyone,' said Ad.

Jackson glared at him, then continued, 'Quite frankly, the only reason I haven't fired you already is that it would complicate things for XPERIENCE, and we have ploughed too much capital into them for this to go south.'

This was horrible. I felt like I was being told off by a teacher.

'One more strike and you're out. Understood?'

I nodded, relieved that I wasn't being sacked. Going back to Tammerstone would be a disaster.

'Now,' he said. 'On to other business. The album is almost in the bag and we're going to want to get it out there as soon as possible. I've had some cover roughs printed.'

Jackson reached into his desk drawer and pulled out a big card square. There was a picture of XPERIENCE on it. Well, I say XPERIENCE, but it was more Greeny, with Harry and Ad way in the background. At the top, in big gold lettering, it said: 'LOL—Love Our Lives—XPERIENCE.

I said nothing. I was on thin ice already.

'This is a bloody joke, right?' said Harry.

'You don't like it?' said Jackson.

'Well of course I don't,' said Harry. 'I mean, "LOL"? I've

never lolled in my life! And what's going on with that photo? Are me and Ad even in it?'

Jackson sniggered. 'I've already told you, Harry. Greeny is the focal point of this band.'

I glanced across at Greeny. He looked like he wanted to die.

'Hang about,' said Ad. 'I thought Joe was supposed to be drawing our album cover.'

'Right now, I wouldn't trust that boy to draw my curtains,' said Jackson.

The room went quiet as a fog of depression descended.

'What if we leave?' said Harry. 'What if we don't want to be associated with you any more?'

Jackson smiled, revealing his small, white teeth.

'Then you will be in breach of contract and liable for all the money we have invested in you.'

'So you'd sue us?' I asked.

He nodded. 'Big time. And we'd take everything, too. You know the lawyer that got Marcy Slick off her drink driving rap, even though she'd crashed her car into a KFC then tried to give Colonel Sanders a hickey? He's on our payroll.'

I gulped.

'So are you with me or not?'

'I suppose we have no choice,' said Harry.

'Damn straight,' said Jackson. 'Now get back into that studio.'

When I got home after a day of shredding old contracts with Horatio, I found Harry, Ad, and Greeny already there. Harry was desperately trying to get through to Verity and Jasmeen but they weren't answering.

'I keep telling you, they're not going to help,' said Greeny.

'And I keep telling you, SHUT UP,' said Harry, jabbing at the keys.

'All right, sorry,' said Greeny.

'As you should be,' Harry fired back. 'Bloody glory hog.'

Greeny looked at me, his mouth open wide. 'You think I want this? I don't want to be the biggest thing on the album cover, regardless of how buff I look.'

Harry groaned and started having a go at Greeny. Ad joined in. I tried to step in to stop them, but they all ignored me. Then Dad walked in.

'Yo, yo, yo, what's with all the beefing?'

'I'll tell you what the bloody beefing is, old son,' said Harry. 'This.'

He held up the mock-up of LOL.

'Woah, bitching cover, yo!' said Dad. He held both hands up for high fives, but was left brutally hanging.

'So what's the plan?' said Dad. 'You just talk to that Jackson playa and he changes it, right?'

'Hardly,' said Harry. 'He intimated that if we went against him, he would sue us and Joe would be sacked.'

Dad nodded and stroked his chin. 'I think there is only

one way we can come up with a solution, yo.'

'What's that?' Ad asked.

'Hot tub conference,' said Dad.

So five minutes later, we were all sitting in the hot tub. Dad was playing some subdued hip-hop and sipping a pina colada. So far, these were the only ideas we'd managed to come up with . . .

DAD: Get some of the rap heavies he has 'befriended' at freestyle events to go in and talk to Jackson.

ME: Hire a gang of master criminals like off *Ocean's Eleven* to break into PGS's vault and destroy the contracts.

AD: Same as mine but with flying monkeys.

GREENY: Fake our deaths and restart our lives in Jamaica.

While we were going through all that, Harry sat silently and stared into space, puffing on a pipe with a contemplative look on his face.

'What are you thinking about, Harry?' I asked him.

Harry took a long drag, then fixed his gaze on me. 'I think I may have a plan, old son.'

Friday 28th February

We stayed up late into the night, planning what we were going to do. The air crackled with excitement. It's been ages since we've carried out one of Harry's strategies. I mean, yes, every time we tried one when we were at school, it ended in disaster, but there was no way this one could fail.

Greeny had pieced together a hacking program and loaded it onto a USB, which was clenched in my sweaty hand as I entered PGS headquarters.

I found Horatio in the small filing room at the other end of the corridor to Jackson's office.

'Good morning, Horatio,' I said.

Horatio winced. 'Not so loud, my good fellow. I am rather suffering from the effects of last night's Châteauneuf-du-Pape.'

« Older posts

'Here's the thing,' I said to him. 'I need your dad's email address.'

Horatio glared at me. 'You're not going to inform on me, are you?'

'No,' I said. 'I just need to do some admin for Jackson, and I don't want to ask him for it, because you know what he's like.'

Horatio rolled his eyes. 'Tell me about it. So touchy. Wouldn't even let me try his wig on.'

He wrote his dad's email on a piece of paper. I thanked him, then turned around and headed into the corridor. I pulled out my phone and texted Harry.

ALPHA LOCATION OBTAINED. BEGIN DECOY PRO-TOCOL.

The reply came back immediately.

ROGER.

I knew what must have been happening at that point. Harry and Greeny would start arguing. Then Ad would join in. Eventually, the argument would become so intense, it would become physical—shoving, pulling to the ground.

Pepe would try to regain control, but the fight would be too much for him and he would—

RRRRRIINNG.

—call Jackson.

I ducked into the supply closet and left the door open just a crack so I could see out. Jackson's door flew open and he stormed down the corridor towards the studio.

I quickly jumped out and ducked into the office, heading straight to Jackson's laptop, USB in hand. I shoved it in the slot, and even got it the right way around at the first attempt.

The program started downloading onto the computer. It was a pretty big file, so it would take a couple of minutes.

Greeny explained how it would work. It would hack into Jackson's email account and send the following pre-written email to Sir Leonard Ampleforth, PGS President and Horatio's dad.

Yo Lenny,

You've given me this XPERIENCE band to work with and, quite frankly, I can't be arsed. They're too advanced for me.

Tell you what I really like—pan-pipe music from Papua New Guinea. You should send me there.

Cheers, sugar-knockers,
Jackson McHugh

Greeny's program would leave no trace that it has come from us, so Jackson wouldn't be able to sack me. It was a foolproof plan.

« Older posts

Then the office door opened.

I yanked the USB out and hit the floor, scooched under the desk and curled into a ball. I felt my phone buzz in my pocket. I twisted around to grab it and take a look.

TARGET LEAVING LOCATION. CLEAR AREA.

Yeah, THANKS.

I breathed in and curled into a tighter ball as Jackson sat back down. His knees were centimetres from my face. If he stretched out, I'd be done for. He'd catch me and this would be the strike he was waiting for.

I heard him pick up his phone.

'Yeah, can I get a security team down in studio two? Got a band in there thinking it's some kind of fight club.'

CRAP! Now even if I text the guys to have another fight, Jackson wouldn't have to move. I was stuck.

Just remain calm, Joe, said Norman. *We'll figure a way out of this.*

Oh, will we? said Hank. *And how are we going to do that, exactly? He's stuck under a desk with his face buried in some guy's crotch. There's no way this could get any worse.*

I heard a rumble. It sounded like distant thunder. But it wasn't thunder. And it wasn't as distant as I would have liked. It travelled down Jackson's belly, moving lower and lower until . . .

PRRRRRRRFFFFFTTT.

Gas attack! Gas attack! Masks on! This is not a drill!

The stench was overpowering. It was like a hundred three-week-old cabbages bobbing in a septic tank.

There had to be a way out. I'd die otherwise. I dashed out a text to Dad:

STUCK UNDER JACKSONS DSK. CALL PGS. MAKE DISTRACTION.

I waited. And waited. No response.

There was nothing else I could do. I wasn't going to text Mila. I'm trying to show her I'm a cool city guy and cool city guys don't get stuck in under-desk stink ovens. No, I would just have to die of methane poisoning.

But then I remembered one last person I could try. A couple of seconds after I pressed send, I had a reply.

COWLEY! How did this happen? You know what, now probably isn't the best time for questions. Hold on.

After a couple of minutes, Jackson's phone rang.

'Jackson McHugh . . . what do you mean, my Lambo's being towed? I have a permit. Hold on.'

He got up and stomped out. As soon as I heard the door slam, I slid out and made my escape. There was no way

« Older posts

I was going to risk him coming back again. I texted Harry.

MISSION FAILED.

Then, I sent Natalie a message.

Thank you so much! How did you know he drove a Lamborghini?

Lucky guess. Can't believe I'm still bailing you guys out. What would you do without me, eh?

I don't know.

Saturday 1st March

I was up early this morning, getting ready to head back to Tammerstone, when Mila called to say she couldn't come.

Apparently, the keyboard player they picked has quit so they have to audition a new one.

It's a good thing she's telling him this on the phone, said Hank.

Why? said Norman.

Cos that way Joe can't see her nose growing.

Yeah well, what does Hank know? Mila would never lie to me, and I know this because she loves me and I trust her implicitly. Plus, I kind of staked out the audition venue on my way to the train station and saw her go in.

So me and Greeny (who gladly received Mila's ticket) arrived back in Tammerstone at about twelve. It was just the same as it ever was—a one-horse town. Not like London. London's got loads of horses. The Queen alone must have a couple of dozen.

All the old sights greeted me: Woodlet High, Paphlos's kebab shop, Mad Morris trying to convert a postbox to Christianity. It felt tired and boring. But at the same time, there was another feeling. Like a painful sensation deep in my belly—and I don't think it was due to the crappy roll I ate on the train. Looking at things like benches stirred it up in me. Then memories came back—that was the bench where Natalie and I had our first and last kisses. I thought about giving her a call while I was in town and seeing if she wanted to meet up for a coffee or something.

Hold your fire, Joe, Norman stopped me.

Aw hell, what now, Norm? said Hank.

Consider your actions very carefully, he said. *Remember how long it took you to get over her before? Do you really want to go down that path again? All that misery and pain?*

Hank shook his head. *You guys overthink everything. He just wants to hit the chick up while he's in town. Dutch girl doesn't even need to know about it.*

Hank is such a sleaze. I sided with Norman and didn't touch my phone. I think my relationship with Natalie is best kept as an online thing. The occasional friendly email—no dramas.

I opened the front door and crept in. I wanted to sneak up on Mum and surprise her.

The house seemed empty even though Mum's car

« Older posts

and Jim's van were outside. I heard noises coming from upstairs, so I quietly made my way up.

The noises were coming from my bedroom. I couldn't make out what they were to begin with, but then it became quite clear. Banging. And panting.

Oh my GOD. Were Gav and Poppy literally doing it in MY bedroom?

No.

It was much worse than that.

'Do it harder, Jim,' Mum moaned. 'Harder!'

Oh you have GOT to be kidding me, said Hank, burying his face in his hands.

Tidal waves of spew surged from my stomach. How the hell could they taint my bedroom in such a way? I mean, I know I don't live there any more but, come on, have some decency.

'I'm banging as hard as I can, woman, are you trying to kill me?' Jim yelled. 'How's things your end, Chips?'

AAAAAAAAAAAAAAAAAAARRRRRRGGHHHH!!!

CHIPS? JIM'S BEST MAN CHIPS? WITH THE YEL-LOW TEETH AND THE BROWN FINGERS AND THE . . . AAAAARRRGGHHH, THIS IS THE MOST DISGUSTING THING THAT HAS EVER HAPPENED!

'It's bloody filthy back here,' Chips grunted. 'You could have given it a wipe first.'

UUGGGGHHHHHH!!!!! TSUNAMIS OF VOMIT!

'That's it!' I screamed. 'Enough! Stop what you're doing and get the hell out of my room.'

The noise stopped and the door opened. The three of them stood there, fully clothed, halfway through trying to dismantle the bunk bed. I have never felt relief like it. But this relief quickly gave way to anger.

'Hey, what are you doing with my bed?'

Mum flew out of my room and grabbed me, peppering my face with kisses. 'Oh, my boy, my baby, my baby boy . . .' etc.

Once she'd finally let me go, I stepped into the room. The mattresses were propped up in the corner. Jim and Chips were sweating. Chips was wearing a stringy vest, which was pretty horrible.

'Oh God, you're not smoking in my room, are you?' I groaned.

'Nah,' said Chips. 'I've turned over a new leaf. I vape now.' He pulled three metal pipes out of his pocket and took a massive drag on all of them at once.

'What's happening to my bed?' I said, inwardly questioning why I was getting so upset about it. I remembered when they first bought it and I had to sleep directly under Gav's noisy arse. I threatened to leave home and everything.

'Well, Gavin has been saving up and has bought himself a nice double bed,' said Mum.

'What?' I cried. 'Why would he need a double bed?'

'I have no idea,' Chips sniggered. Jim joined in, but Mum shot him one of her lethal looks and he stopped.

'Well what a turn up for the cocking books this is!' I said. 'Where am I supposed to sleep?'

'We've thought of that, you silly sausage,' said Mum.

She led me into the twins' room and showed me a sofa bed.

'Great,' I said. 'I get to stay with a couple of screaming, pooing lunatics.'

'Joe,' Mum snapped. 'That's your sisters you're talking about. Besides, we weren't expecting you back. We thought you'd be in London a while longer.'

I huffed and folded my arms. 'I wanted to surprise you. Wish I hadn't bothered now.'

Mum grabbed me and kissed my cheek again. 'Don't be such a drama queen. We'll have a lovely family dinner tonight. Anyway, Gavin and Poppy have taken the twins over to the park. Why don't you go and find them? They'll be thrilled to see you.'

When I got to the park, I saw Gav and Poppy sitting on a bench, kissing. Nice to see they're as revoltingly in love as ever. Holly and Ivy were running around in their little bear coats, completely unsupervised. They could have been carried off by a hawk or anything.

When Holly saw me, she yelled, 'OH!' and ran at me, her arms outstretched. Ivy joined her. She fell over en route, but picked herself straight back up, and I knelt down to hug them. They bellowed right down my ear and accidentally punched me in the face a couple of times, but it was nice to see them again.

Poppy ran over and bear hugged me when I stood up.

'Oh, Joey-Joe-Joe, it's sooo great to see you! To begin with, I thought some random stranger was hugging the girls, but when I saw it was you, I was so relieved and . . . ooh, how's London? Is it exciting? The last time I was there I saw a tramp fighting a flock of pigeons. It was quite distressing. Oh, Schmuffycakes, Joe is here—come and give him a hug.'

Gav got up slowly and nodded at me. 'Aight, bruv.'

'Whatever,' I said. 'Congratulations, by the way.'

Gav and Poppy gave each other a quick look. 'What for?'

'Taking my room from me,' I said. 'It took you a couple of years but you finally managed it.'

Gav looked all sheepish and stared at the floor. Poppy just laughed, though.

'Oh, Joey-Joe-Joe, you are so FUNNY. You HAVE to come with us to the party tonight.'

I could tell Gav was sending her silent 'shut up' vibes, but they weren't getting through.

'What party is this?' I asked.

'A boy I know from college. I think his name's James, or John, or Jimbo. I don't know. Anyway, I could totally bring you as my guest of honour.'

I chuckled to myself. 'I'll stay at home, thanks. I hardly think a college party is going to live up to all the swanky London galas I've been attending.'

NINE HOURS LATER

'That's it, I'm going.'

'Huh? Why?' Mum asked.

'Well, as much as I'd love to stay and watch old home movies of two-year-old me singing Mr Tumble songs with my knob out, I've got somewhere to be.'

Mum stopped rooting through the cabinet and looked up at me. 'Where are you going?'

'Gav and Poppy invited me to a party,' I said. 'Sorry, I have to spend time with everyone, it's only fair.'

'You're right,' said Mum. 'As much as I want my baby boy all to myself, he has to get out there and be a man.' She gave me my fifty-millionth kiss of the day. 'I'll make the sofa bed up. Just try not to disturb the twins when you come in.'

Gav texted me the address of the house. It was one of the big, posh places on Gillcroft Lane. There was a string of coloured lanterns hanging above the doorway, and the sounds of music and excited talking drifted out of the open door. Straight away, my old eye twitch came back. *Is there* anything worse than walking into a party alone? What do you do? Say hello to people? What if they don't say hello back? What if I think I've said hello, but I've actually said, 'You smell like wee and biscuits?' What if I DIE?

I tried to put all the panicky thoughts out of my head and stride into that party as confidently as I could. What do I have to be afraid of? I am a cosmopolitan city boy. I've been to parties that have FONDUE. These small town hicks won't be able to handle my awesomeness.

I walked inside. It was rammed. I vaguely recognized a couple of people from school. The kinds of people who used to hold doors open for me, then pretend to slam them in my face and laugh when I screamed. I kept my head down and carried on walking. I just wanted to find Gav and Poppy.

When I did, I wished I hadn't.

'I love YOU more.'

'No I love YOOUUU more, Schmuffycakes.'

'No I love YOOOUUUU.'

I cleared my throat. Gav stood up straight, scratched his head and nodded at me. 'All right?'

'Will be,' I said. 'As soon as I've finished throwing up my entire digestive tract.'

At least the party was better than sitting through old home movies. Just about. Hanging around with a couple is no fun, though. They've got all these little in-jokes. Poppy tried to explain them to me, but they were mostly very you-had-to-be-there.

I decided to go for a walk outside. The party was already giving me a headache.

I noticed a small outbuilding with the light switched on. I thought I'd go and investigate. Generally, my kind of people like to find somewhere to hide at parties, so I thought I might find some kindred spirits there. Maybe we could while the night away talking **STAR TREK** or playing D&D.

I stood on my tiptoes and took a peek through the window. There was a couple in there. The lad was leaning against a cupboard, his eyes closed and his head tilted back, while the girl went to town on his neck.

Ugh. There was no way I was going in there. It was bad enough being the third wheel for Gav and Poppy, let alone some couple I didn't know.

I was about to walk away when the lad's eyes shot open and he looked straight at me.

Oh. Bum.

'What do you think you're doing?'

He came flying out of the building and pushed me. I stumbled backwards and landed arse-first on a wet barbeque.

'Are you some kind of pervert, is that it? I won't have misogynist creeps in my house!'

'Jez, come on, leave it.' I heard the girl emerge behind him. As soon as her voice registered in my brain, alarm bells rang and the control room, already on high alert, went code red.

No freakin' way, said Hank.

It *can't be!* said Norman. *I've requested confirmation, but the voice recognition department has shut down!*

'Not cool, man,' said the lad, running a hand through his curly hair.

The girl stood next to him and put her arm around his shoulders to try to calm him down. Then she saw me.

'Oh my God—JOE?'

I blinked hard. The girl in front of me sounded like Natalie, even looked like Natalie, but she had changed. A lot.

She wasn't wearing make-up and her hair was light brown—her natural colour. She was wearing a white T-shirt, green hoodie, and khaki trousers.

'Oh, this is your ex, isn't it?' said the boy, pulling at a grotty wristband on his arm.

Natalie laughed nervously. 'Bloody hell, Cowley.'

'I'm sorry,' I said, trying to do something to stop the feeling that I might burst into hysterical tears. 'I was just seeing who was in here. I had no idea it would be you. Doing *that*.'

Natalie sighed and rubbed Jez's arm. 'He's not lying, Jez. Stuff like this happens to Joe. All the time.'

I nodded. 'It's like a disease.'

Jez shook his head and stuck his hand out. I shook it. 'I'm sorry, man,' he said. 'I shouldn't have shoved you like that. Are you OK?'

'Um, yeah I'm fine.'

We all stood there, dead awkward. I looked back towards the house, hoping for some kind of distraction. Nothing.

'So,' said Natalie. 'I didn't know you were back from London. What happened—did the music thing not work out?'

I frowned. The music thing? Why was she being so vague?

'No, as I said in my em—'

Natalie's eyes went wide and she shook her head slightly.

« Older posts

'Em . . . otional Facebook post, we've got to carry on because of our contract. I just came back for the weekend to see family.'

Natalie smiled and nodded. It went awkward again.

'You look . . .'

'Different?'

'Well, yeah.'

'Yeah, I don't dye my hair any more.'

'Oh. Why's that?'

'Man,' said Jez, shaking his head. 'If you knew what chemicals they put in that stuff, it would turn your stomach. It's like they don't care what they're doing to the environment. Makes me sad.'

His face went all weepy and he looked at the floor. Natalie rubbed his back. 'It's OK, Jez.'

Oh give me a freakin' break, said Hank. *He's like that crying Native American guy.*

Well that's just being insensitive, said Norman.

I wonder what his tribe name is? said Hank, *ignoring him. Big Chief Kisses Your Ex?*

'Well, Jez,' I said. 'It was nice meeting you, and, again, sorry about the . . .' I nodded at the outhouse.

'That's all right,' he replied. 'Sorry about the . . .' He made a shoving gesture.

I looked at Natalie. 'It was nice . . .'

She nodded and smiled. 'Yeah. Keep in . . .'

One of these days someone is going to finish a sentence around here, said Hank.

I went home and lay on the sofa bed. I know I've got Mila and I shouldn't feel like this, but seeing Natalie with that Jez literally KILLED ME TO DEATH.

I've just been cyberstalking him to look for some kind of flaw, but he has none. He volunteers in a soup kitchen for the homeless for crying out loud! The closest thing I've ever come to that is when Mad Morris chased me with a Bible and I threw a Pot Noodle at him.

And he's fit. I mean, I don't find boys attractive or anything, but I can totally see it. Muscular, deep blue eyes, dreamy smile. For Natalie, that's like going from a rickshaw to a Bentley. The upgrade of the century.

I've just googled his name again and seen a fundraising page for a triathlon he's doing to raise money for endangered animals. There's a link to a Tammerstone Times article about it, too. Here we go . . . 'Precocious Jeremy, a Grade 8 piano player, who has represented the county at rugby and hopes to become a maxillofacial surgeon, fixing

« Older posts

children's cleft palates in the Indian subcontinent, is pas-
sionate about preserving wildlife.'

UGGGHHHHHHH!

2 a.m.

Had to stop mid groan there because my InstaMsg
beeped and came dangerously close to waking the twins.
It was from Natalie. I switched it to silent and read.

**Sorry I didn't tell you abt Jez. Didn't know proper
way to bring it up. Plus, stuff like that can make you a
bit . . .**

Mental?

Yeah. You're not upset are you?

Why would I be upset?

. . . I don't know.

So . . . how did you meet?

College.

**OK. You're all right with the whole hair-dying thing,
aren't you?**

**Course I am. I'd be selfish to carry on doing that,
wouldn't I?**

**I don't know. As long as he's not forcing you to
change.**

**He's not . . . thanks for being so mature about this,
though.**

That's OK, I'm not as idiotic as I used to be.

Do keep emailing, Cowley. I enjoy hearing what you've been up to. You might have guessed that Jez doesn't know about it.

Yeah, I got that impression.

I don't know why. I'm pretty sure he wouldn't mind. It's just . . . I don't know, it's late and I'm tired.

Me too. Night, Natalie.

Night, Cowley. X

Monday 3rd March

Just before I headed back to London yesterday, I saw Gav and Poppy at breakfast. After trying to be subtle about it, I came right out with it.

'So, this Jez, then,' I said. 'You know him?'

'Not really,' said Poppy. 'I mean, I see him about a bit, what with him being in the ads for New Power Gym.'

'What?!'

'Oh yeah,' she said. 'That's him on the side of all the buses. Sooo ripped.'

Gav cleared his throat, and Poppy suddenly turned and grabbed him. 'But I don't like six packs, I prefer a little more junk in the trunk, isn't that right, Schmuffycakes?'

I took that as my cue to leave. I mean, a bloody model.

Anyway, after a LONG morning of delivering mail to various unpleasant people around the building and

« Older posts

washing Jackson's Lamborghini, Mila turned up at the office. Her boss had given her the afternoon off, so she was free to go for lunch with me.

We were hoping to try Harry's strategy again but XPERIENCE were under closer watch in the studio and Jackson never left his room.

Me and Mila ended up at a cafe around the corner. It's pretty much the same as Griddler's in Tammerstone, except they charge four quid for a bacon butty. I mean, how can they justify that? Is it made from Peppa Pig or something?

Sorry, I'm in a bad mood at the moment. AND HERE'S WHY.

MILA: Joe, I've got something to tell you.

ME (inwardly freaking out that she's dumping me): Oh really? Well, that's interesting. I mean, are you sure? Sometimes it's best not to. Just keep it bottled up inside. Keep it in until you've completely forgotten what it was. This bacon sandwich is delicious and not at all overpriced.

MILA: Joe, please stop freaking out.

ME: Freaking out? I'm not freaking out. I'm not freaking in either. In fact, I'm not freaking full stop.

MILA (sighing): My bosses have asked me if I want to continue interning for them during the Marcy Slick tour.

ME: OK.

MILA: And I've said yes.

ME: That's fine. So they'll go on tour and you'll carry on working in Ealing?

MILA (putting her hand on mine): Joe. I'm going on tour with them.

ME (trying to drown out the explosion of sadness, fear, and confusion in my brain): Tour? T-tour? I mean . . . how long?

MILA: I'm not sure. It depends how successful it is. Minimum three weeks. Maximum six months.

ME: Sssix months? That's like half a year or something. W-why though? Why tour?

MILA: I guess I'm just a little jealous of Verity and Jasmeen travelling without me. I want to get out and see more of this country. I mean, some of the places on the itinerary

« Older posts

sound so magical . . . Wol-ver-hamp-ton.

ME: Wolverhampton is not magical! Unless you count the time I went there and my phone disappeared out of my pocket!

MILA: I'm sorry, Joe. This is just something I have to do.

Something she has to do? HAS to do? I've looked it up and the only things humans HAVE to do are eat, sleep, and expel waste. Nowhere on that list is disappearing off to Wolverhampton with a pop star who is married to a goat!

Norman tried to calm me down, saying stuff like, *It's OK, Joe. She just wants to get out there and have an experience. She'll come back to you.*

That made me feel better for the two seconds it took for Hank to throw his empty beer can at the wall and stand up.

Right. Just forget about how your buddies' girls never reply to their texts cos they're always hanging out with 'boys'.

That's when it hit me—she isn't jealous of the travelling. She's jealous of the good-looking men she could be hanging around with.

I have to stop this.

12.30 a.m.

You know what? No. I can see myself disappearing into my old obsessive mindset, and I'm putting a stop to it.

If touring is what Mila wants to do, then she has my full blessing.

Wednesday 4th March

OK, so I spent all day yesterday organizing **Operation Persuade Mila to Stay Without Actually Begging** or **OPMSWAB** for short.

See, the way I look at it is, London is a hugely multicultural place. In our building alone, we have people from India (Dr Kunal), Nigeria (Ms Disemi), and Mars (Ad). So why leave? You can experience all the world has to offer without having to set foot outside Zone 6.

Here's the itinerary I have planned for tonight.

5.30 p.m.

Meet Mila at La Araña tapas bar near her office. Make sure there is a selection of Spanish appetisers waiting for her.

7.30 p.m.

Catch a performance of an Israeli experimental opera at the Free Spirit Theatre on the King's Road. This has a dual purpose because, according to Google maps, it is near the

« Older posts

Chelsea ground and they are playing West Bromwich Albion tonight, so hopefully Mila will see their fans and realize that the Black Country isn't as enchanted as she thinks.

9 p.m.

Head back to the flat where I will prepare a romantic lobster meal which I've had to sell some old Xbox games to pay for.

Of course, the meal will be conditional on me having the flat to myself. Which isn't going to be easy.

'I know what this is about,' said Harry, when I asked the three of them if they would make themselves scarce for a couple of hours. 'You want us out of the way so you can play hide the sausage.'

Classy as ever.

'Ah wicked,' said Ad. 'Can I play?'

Harry chuckled. 'I don't think your presence will be appreciated, old son.'

'Yeah it will,' said Ad. 'I used to play hide the sausage all the time with my dad.'

I facepalmed.

'Did you really?' said Harry, barely able to keep himself together.

'Yeah,' said Ad, with a big grin. 'This once, we even let the dog join in.'

I should point out, blog, that Ad's dad is a butcher and not a monster.

'Fine, we'll do you a favour,' said Harry. 'The new *Captain America* is out so we can go and watch that.'

'Yay,' said Greeny, with all the enthusiasm of a dead sloth.

'Thank you,' I said. 'But it's not like that. We're just having a quiet dinner together.'

'You can't fool me, old son,' said Harry. 'I can tell when you're nervous. Your eye twitches; your hands go all fidgety. You'd make a bloody useless spy.'

I tried to stop moving, but that just made me worse. He's right. I'd be a crap Bond.

'OK, I am a bit agitated,' I said. 'But it's not for the reason you think.'

The three of them looked at each other, then Harry put his hand

on my shoulder.

'I think I know why you're scared,' he said.

'Really?' I asked, wondering if Harry had got so good at reading me that he could literally see into my brain. Maybe he had some insight into my problems that could really help me out. 'What is it?'

Harry smiled sympathetically. 'It's your micropenis.'

OK, maybe he didn't have insight after all.

'Oh shut up,' I said, over Greeny and Ad giggling like a couple of idiots. 'I do not have a micropenis. What is a micropenis?'

Harry pulled out his phone and tapped out a Google search, before turning it around and showing me the most horrendous image I have ever seen in my life.

'What do you think, old son?' he said. 'Like looking in a crotch mirror, isn't it?'

Before I could slap him, Dad strutted in.

'Couldn't help but overhear, yo. I guess you want your old dad to bounce, too, so you can get jiggy wit' it.'

Hank and Norman hid behind their clipboards.

'Oh for God's sake,' I said. 'We're not getting jiggy with anything. We're eating lobster.'

'Euphemism,' Harry muttered.

Dad held up his hands. 'You don't have to lie to me, dawg. Hey, I've got something that might help.'

He went to a drawer and pulled out a book.

'This has given me so many tips over the years,' he said, putting it in my hands. 'In fact, you might say that without it you wouldn't be here.'

I dropped the book and wiped my hands down my trousers.

'Wicked,' said Ad, picking it up. 'Can I borrow it?'

'Go nuts, bro,' said Dad. 'I even made some notes in the margins.'

Ad turned it over in his hands as if it was the Holy Grail. 'The key to Joe's mum's heart,' he whispered.

TL;DR . . . They all agreed to disappear for the evening, and if I ever see that book again, I might puke out my own brains.

12.45 a.m.

I left work at lunch today so I could get everything ready. Horatio said he'd cover for me, which didn't exactly fill me with confidence because the other day he completely forgot who I was.

I cleaned the flat, put together a romantic Spotify playlist, and picked up the lobster from the shop. When the woman passed it to me in the box, I thought she was trolling me.

'You are aware this is still alive, aren't you?'

« Older posts

She scowled at me as if I'd just dropped my kecks and rubbed my bare arse on a halibut.

'Yes,' she said. 'We only sell live lobsters. You must cook them that way.'

'What, alive?' I said. 'Doesn't that hurt?'

'I've not heard one complain yet.'

I didn't know if I had it in me to kill a lobster, but I guessed I was just going to have to suck it up and do it. I put it in the cupboard where it would be nice and cool.

Later, I stepped into La Araña and took a deep breath. I wanted to set the tone for the evening by buying Mila a glass of wine before she arrived. The barman had other ideas.

'ID,' he grunted.

'ID? Is that one of those new alcopops?' I said, with what was supposed to be a cool laugh but actually sounded more like a sheep falling off a cliff. 'No, a glass of your finest red, please.'

The barman crossed his arms. 'How old are you?'

Tell him you're thirty, said Hank. *Dream big.*

He'll never believe that, said Norman. *Go for nineteen.*

Anyway, he was staring at me and I was just standing there moving my lips, so I ended up saying, 'Thirfteen.'

'You're *thirteen*?' he said.

'No, I'm . . .' I stopped and looked around. 'Look, mate.'

Upon hearing me call him mate, he made a face like

I had just licked my finger and stuck it in his earhole. I pressed on regardless.

'I'm going to be completely honest with you—I'm seventeen. The wine is not for me. It is for my nineteen-year-old girlfriend who will be here any minute now. Tonight is kind of an important night for me, and I wanted to buy her a drink to start it off. Can you do this for me please? I honestly, swear to God, will not touch a drop of it.'

The barman uncrossed his arms and leaned on the bar. He smiled slightly. I knew he looked like a reasonable man.

'I'll do you a Coke and a pack of Wine Gums, how does that sound?'

So that was embarrassing, but the Wine Gums were mostly red and black, so there's that. I also ordered a few plates of tapas. Now, I don't really know what tapas is. The bloke explained to me that it's small portions of food, meant to be shared. I got something called patatas bravas, which it turns out is a fancy term for roast spuds, and some other veggie-type things. I thought it was a pretty sophisticated selection that would hopefully prove that there's no need to leave London.

I sat with my plates and waited. And waited. I glanced at the big clock above the bar. She was fifteen minutes late. That's OK. The auditions were probably running over a bit.

The door opened and she walked in, laughing. This bloke followed her. He was tall and blond, with a beard and

« Older posts

a straw hat on. He looked kind of familiar, too. Like he could have been one of those buskers you see at Tube stations or something.

'Oh hey, Joe!' Mila yelled, forgetting her indoor voice. 'This is Kristoff—he was just auditioning. We're going up to the bar—do you want anything?'

'Um, no thanks.'

I watched as the two of them walked up to the bar together. Kristoff said something which made Mila laugh and touch his shoulder.

We have shoulder contact, said Hank. *This is bad. I'm*

going to initiate a fight sequence.

Norman slapped Hank's hand away from the controls. *You know as well as I do how tactile Mila is. He's probably just going to have one drink with them and then leave.*

'Oh wow,' said Kristoff, as they sat down. 'I love patatas bravas. Say, Joe, how come you didn't order calamari?'

I shrugged, ignoring Hank's screams of, *Cos we didn't know you were coming, did we, ya jerk?*

'I saw it on the menu, but didn't fancy it.'

'Why not, man?' said Kristoff, his eyes all wide like a five year old. 'It's delish.'

'Well,' I said, 'it sounds like what Mola Ram says in Temple of Doom when he's about to rip someone's heart out. So, to be honest, I was worried it was going to be some kind of internal organ.'

Kristoff stared at me for ages, then started laughing.

'You're a real cut-up, Joe,' he said. 'I get what Mila sees in you now.'

Hey, what's that supposed to mean, you hippy? said Hank.

'You'll have to excuse me, Joe,' said Kristoff, maybe sensing that I slightly wanted to smash the plate of patatas bravas in his face. 'I'm kinda giddy cos I just got the gig!'

I looked at Mila. 'The gig?'

'The committee picked Kristoff to be Marcy Slick's keyboard player for the tour,' she said. 'How awesome is that?'

« Older posts

Oh, said Norman.

'So that's definite, is it?' I said. 'No more people to audi-tion?'

'I'm their guy,' said Kristoff. 'So it looks like the two of us are going to be hanging out on the road.'

THIS CANNOT HAPPEN! Hank yelled. *Commence OPMSWAB, stat!*

'Well, we really must be going soon,' I said, tapping my Enterprise watch, then pulling my sleeve over it because I didn't want to look like a nerd. 'Mila and me are going to see some Israeli theatre.'

Kristoff grimaced. 'Israeli theatre? Man, that is geopolit-ically problematic.'

I'll tell you what's problematic, Hank yelled, *my boot in your ass!*

'Yeah, it totally is,' said Mila. 'Joe, I didn't know about this.'

I shrugged, feeling like the world's biggest chump. Why couldn't I have found a play from a country with no prob-lems, like Switzerland or Canada?

I tried to hint that maybe we could leave and do some-thing else, but I went completely ignored and we were still sitting there an hour later. The two of them had spent the whole time drinking and laughing. Always laughing. When Kristoff went up to the bar, he asked if he could get me anything, and I noticed the barman staring at me, so I had to ask for a Diet Coke again.

'Isn't he TOTALLY GREAT?' Mila whisper-shouted.

'Yeah,' I said. 'If by "great" you mean "bum" and by "totally" you mean . . . "hole".'

Mila frowned. 'So, he's "hole bum"?'

Hank and Norman facepalmed.

'Yeah,' I said. 'Exactly.'

Mila laughed. 'Oh, don't be such a grouch. It's THE Kristoff from the Jingle Jangles, and he's sitting with us! I'm trying so hard not to be star-struck.'

I put down my pen. I was doodling pictures of me kicking Kristoff in the nuts on the back of a feedback card.

'The Jingle who?'

Mila whacked my arm. 'I hope you're kidding.'

My laugh caught in my throat. 'Yeah, course I am.'

Mila smiled and ran her finger around the rim of her empty glass. 'Good, because they are the band that soundtracked our special moment.'

Ah, the Jingle Jangles, of course! They were playing at *BUZZFEST* when I drew that picture of Mila on a burger tray. We had that weird moment where we nearly kissed but didn't because I was still obsessed with Natalie. Mila probably sees them as really important to our relationship. They probably sing our song, for crying out loud.

Kristoff turned around and waved at us. Mila beamed and waved back.

« Older posts

'I'm so pleased for him,' she said to me. 'Since the Jingles split, he's been without a gig.'

He came back to the table. 'One Merlot for me,' he said. 'One Shiraz for Mila, and one, um, Diet Coke for Josh.'

'Joe,' I said. 'My name is Joe.'

He laughed as he sat back down. 'Sorry, man. My best buddy back in NYC is called Joe, and you're just so different to him.'

'NYC, eh?' I said. 'So what brings you here?'

Kristoff took a sip of his drink and leaned forward. 'Love Europe. Love the music, love the culture, love the women.' He winked at me. 'If I could get set up over here, I'd be happy as Larry.'

'Great,' I said, making more of an effort to be nice, even though all I wanted to do was kick him out of there, so we could get back to the flat and eat lobster. 'So . . . how do you like it so far?'

'Pretty cool,' he said. 'London's a hell of a town. Can't wait to get over to Amsterdam, though.'

Mila gasped. 'Really? That's my hometown!'

'No way!' Kristoff turned around so he was facing her. 'I've never been, but I see it as my spiritual home. My parents are from there. They taught me Dutch.'

Mila shoved him and said something in Dutch. He laughed and said something back in Dutch, and within seconds, they were in full flow. It was horrible. I felt like Picard when he was stuck on El-Adrel IV with Dathon. I even started saying 'Darmok and Jalad at Tanagre' to myself.

Ah, Natalie would have appreciated that, said Norman.

Yeah, maybe you should email her, said Hank.

I put my hand in my pocket.

Wait, Norman stopped me. *Let's not complicate things. You need all your concentration for what's going on in front of you.*

'Mila?'

They stopped and turned to me. Kristoff looked kind of annoyed.

'What's the matter, Joe?'

'We really do need to get going, don't we?'

She frowned at me as if she didn't know what I was talking about. Which, to be fair, she didn't.

'I've got a surprise for you,' I said. 'At the flat.'

She sighed. 'OK. We'll go when I've finished this drink.'

I looked at her glass. She'd hardly touched it. In fact, by the time she'd finished it, we were the only ones left in the bar. Kristoff finally left us, with a handshake for me and what I thought was an uncomfortably long hug for Mila.

'So,' said Mila, turning to me and smiling, 'you have a surprise for me?'

I looked at my phone. 'It's eleven. Everyone will be back now.'

'So?'

« Older posts

'So I'd organized a romantic lobster dinner for the two of us.'

Mila clasped her hands to her face. 'Oh, Joe, I'm so sorry,' she said. 'Why didn't you say something?'

'I tried,' I said. 'You were too busy yakking it up with your boyfriend.'

Mila put her hand on my shoulder. 'Don't be that way, Joe. I promise, I'll make it up to you before I leave.'

The only way she could make it up to me is to not leave in the first place. Oh, this was the worst night ever. She's going to be spending every night with that keyboard-playing, hat-wearing, opinions-about-global-politics-having MORON and I'm going to be stuck in London, shuffling papers with Lord Braindead of Idiotshire.

When I got back, sure enough, everyone was home. Dad was in his bedroom doing a hip-hop aerobics workout video with the door open and Harry and Greeny were watching a film in the living room.

I went into the cupboard for the lobster. I was going to try to take it back to the shop tomorrow morning for a refund. But it wasn't there.

'Um, guys?'

'Looking for your lobster?' said

Greeny.

'Yes.'

'Go and see Ad,' said Harry. 'You won't believe your eyes.'

No! Surely Ad hadn't eaten the lobster that cost more than Epic Warfare IV: Deluxe Package. I went straight into his room without knocking, which is normally a risky strategy, but I was too angry to care.

The room was dark when I walked in, except for what looked like torchlight under Ad's duvet. I could hear his voice. It was quiet and he seemed to be reading something.

'Massage the area sense . . . sense you . . . sens-u-all-y until your lover starts to purr. Ugh, that'd be like doing it with a cat.'

I turned the light on and took in the scene. Ad was lying on his stomach under the duvet, reading *The Art of Love* to my lobster.

'What the hell are you doing?' I yelled.

Ad shot up and glared at me, his eyes massive behind his glasses. 'I can't believe you were going to kill Sebastian!'

My mouth dropped open. 'SEBASTIAN?'

'Yeah, I've named him,' said Ad. 'My favourite film is *The Little Mermaid.*'

I couldn't believe what I was hearing. 'One,' I said. 'Since when is your favourite film *The Little* bloody *Mermaid*? Two, Sebastian is a crab not a lobster. Three, I can't believe you'd name it after the moron who split me and Natalie up and made my life miserable. And four, I'm taking that lobster back tomorrow.'

Ad snatched up the lobster and held it, stroking along its horrible carapace while it clacked its pincers contentedly.

'No way,' he said. 'If you take that back someone else will buy him and eat him. And I don't want Sebastian to get eaten. We've been bonding, haven't we, Sebastian?'

I can't believe how much has changed in such a short time. One minute we're in the woods pretending to be Jedis, the next we're in London reading sex manuals to lobsters.

Thursday 6th March

I barely slept last night. Mostly because I was trying to figure out a way of stopping this whole Mila/Kristoff situation and partly because I could hear Ad singing to Sebastian through the wall.

Harry wants to have another go at sending the abusive email to the PGS President and I've told him I'll try, but secretly I have a new priority. I have to get Kristoff off this tour. I know there's no way I can get Mila to leave. It has to be him.

And look, blog, I refuse to feel guilty about this. He is quite clearly a nasty piece of work. I mean, he totally froze me out last night—made me look stupid, spoke Dutch so I couldn't join in. And he can always get another job. Maybe Tammerstone Church needs an organist.

Right. It's time to sabotage a career.

8.15 p.m.

I am the WORST at sabotage.

I snuck away from restocking the teabags and went into the courtyard. Making sure no one was around, I dialled the Ealing office. I took a deep breath and closed my eyes.

'Good morning, PGS?'

'Yah, hi there . . . buddy,' I said in the best New York accent I could manage. 'I gotta talk to the guy in charge of Marcy's band.'

The line went quiet.

'OK, who shall I say is calling?'

Ah, thank Jesus, she didn't hang up.

'Kristoff,' I said. 'Kristoff . . .'

You didn't find out his last name did you, genius? said Hank.

'Kristoff the keyboard guy,' I said. 'They'll know who

you're talking about.'

'One moment, please.'

The line cut off and an old Marcy Slick ballad played. I remember they always used to play it as the slowie at school discos. Which means I will forever associate it with standing at the edge of a room, sipping squash and getting depressed about Lisa Hall.

'Perry Wyndham?'

"Sup, Perry, it's Kristoff,' I said. 'I was just calling to say I want off your crappy tour and that you stink of dookie.'

He didn't speak. All I could hear was his breath on the other side, slow and measured. After what felt like an aeon, he spoke.

'Kristoff is here in the office. Who is this?'

BUMMMMMMMMMMMMMM!!

'Sorry,' I said. 'I am . . . his evil twin. Who has the same name as him. Bye!'

I hung up quickly before I could say anything else ridiculous.

Later on I called Mila to make sure she hadn't got wind of what had happened. Surely if she had, she would put two and two together.

'Heyyy, this is Mila,' said a voice that definitely wasn't Mila.

I heard her giggling in the background. 'Kristoff, stop

that! You're such a klootzak!'

'Hey, that's no way to speak to your secretary.'

As my anger levels began to go volcanic, I heard Mila wrestle the phone away from Kristoff.

'Hey, Joe!'

'What's going on?' I said. 'Why's he answering your phone?'

'Oh, he's just being silly. We were having a break and Kristoff was teaching me to play keyboard. He says I'm a natural.'

'I bet he does,' I said through teeth so gritted they were almost ground into powder.

'He's going to give me some more lessons when we're on tour,' she went on. 'Isn't he a nice guy?'

'The nicest,' I said, folding a piece of paper into a dagger shape.

When I got home, Harry and Greeny were lying face down on the sofa. Ad was in the hot tub with Sebastian.

'Bad day at the studio?'

'I'm thinking of running away,' said Greeny, all muffled by a cushion. 'I mean, they can't sue someone they can't find, can they?'

Harry sat up and massaged his temples.

'They told us today that "Kamikaze Attack" and "Dive, Dive, Dive" aren't going to be on the album. Instead, there

« Older posts

will be a salsa remix of "Gay as the Day Is Long" and a karaoke version. I tried to get to McHugh to talk to Pepe, but the security wouldn't let me past.'

'It's all a nightmare,' said Greeny. 'This whole thing is HELL.'

Ad leaned over the side of the tub.

'It ain't all that bad.'

'What are you talking about, old son?'

'It's different now,' he said. 'I've got Sebastian. Since my dog Chunky died, I've always wanted a new pet.'

He picked Sebastian up and laughed as he tried to clamp down on his glasses. 'Ooh, you're a cheeky boy,' he said. 'Yes you are!'

'That reminds me, old son,' said Harry. 'Turn the temperature of that tub down now or you'll be making the world's biggest pot of lobster bisque.'

God, everything about this is a nightmare. It was supposed to be a time of change—I was going to become a sophisticated city man, with a cool girlfriend, making my way in the record business. As it stands, my girlfriend is leaving with some guy she idolizes, my career is already in the toilet and I'm sharing a flat with my tragic dad, two miserable bandmates, and one who has gone so mental, he's befriended a crustacean.

There has to be a solution to all of this, but it'd take some kind of mega genius to figure it out.

Friday 7th March

Maybe I really am a mega genius.

OK, maybe that's going a bit too far. I'm certainly some kind of genius, though.

I was in the middle of refreshing the magazines in the waiting room when Jackson stuck his head around his door.

'Joe, I'm going to need three espressos, now.'

Then he disappeared back inside, slamming the door behind him.

I did as I was told and carried the three little mugs into his office, putting them down on the desk in front of him. Without looking up, Jackson downed the first one.

'OW!'

Then the second.

'OW!'

Then the third.

'OWWWWWWW CRAP!'

He collapsed forward onto his desk, burying his face in his arms.

'Um, is everything OK?'

Jackson looked up, his face a mixture of tired and furious.

'The Clean League have pulled out of the Marcy Slick tour that starts next week.'

'OK,' I said. 'Can you not just hire another cleaning agency?'

Jackson screwed his eyes shut. 'Remind me how you got a job in the music industry again? The Clean League are one of the hottest bands on our roster and I've just found out they can't do the tour because their lead singer has checked into rehab. I mean, what a WUSS!'

Yeah, he's a really understanding sort of bloke.

'Where am I going to find a support act at such short notice?' he said. 'President Ampleforth's going to have my ass on a platter.'

I wasn't going to offer to help him. In fact, this might have solved our problem without me having to do anything. If Ampleforth sacked him, we could have been on easy street.

But then another thought occurred to me. Something that could solve a different problem. I stood there, staring dumbly while my brain went backwards and forwards.

I could sort out the XPERIENCE problem or the Mila problem.

XPERIENCE or Mila.

X or M.

Just had a thought, said Hank.

That sounds dangerous, said Norman.

Shut it, Norm, said Hank. *Listen, kid. If you take care of the Mila problem, it will sort the Dad problem, too.*

'Hey!' Jackson snapped his fingers at me. 'Dum-dum! What are you staring at?'

'I have a suggestion,' I said.

He looked at me sceptically, but pointed at a chair anyway. I guess he must have been desperate.

I sat down and double-checked with the control room that this was really what I wanted to do.

'You say you haven't got a support act for the Marcy Slick tour,' I said. 'I say, if you walk down the corridor and enter recording studio two, you will find one.'

Jackson stared at me open-mouthed. Then he laughed. Hard. He even banged the table with his fist.

'You think your boys should be the opening act for Marcy Slick?' he roared. 'Are you TRIPPING?'

'I promise you they're ready,' I said.

'Ready?' he cried. 'The only thing those clowns are ready for is the Job Centre. Yesterday I went down there and the stupid one was FaceTiming with a crab!'

'It's actually a lobster,' I said. 'But that's beside the point. Look, they can do it. Don't forget—performing live was how they got their reputation in the first place. They will smash it.'

« Older posts

Jackson frowned. 'You really think so?'

I nodded. 'That's what's wrong with them. They're hungry for the roar of the crowd. Once you get them out there with the people, the album will follow straight away.'

He sighed. 'I don't know—it's a hell of a risk.'

'It isn't,' I said. 'But if it all goes wrong, I will take full responsibility. I will go with them on the road and help keep them in line.'

Jackson sat back in his chair and stared at the ceiling.

HMMMMM

'They would be a lot cheaper than the Clean League.'

'The cheapest,' I said. 'Just give them a chance.'

He sat forward again and stared at me. His eyes were so piercing, they almost took my attention away from his daft hair.

'Fine,' he said. 'But this goes wrong and it's your ass, not mine.'

'My ass,' I said.

Jackson's face slowly broke into a smile as he shook my hand. 'You got yourself a deal.'

I smiled, too. Not because I was excited about going on tour, or because I wasn't terrified about telling the guys. I just couldn't wait to see Kristoff's face when he finds out he's not going to be teaching my girlfriend keyboard every night. Stick that up your geopolitically problematic arse, you beardy knobber!

Saturday 8th March

'NO! NO, NO NOOOO!'

Greeny ran into his bedroom, slamming the door shut behind him and making the light go off.

So basically, me telling the guys they will be supporting Marcy Slick on tour went about as well as I expected.

'How has this happened, old son?' said Harry.

I shrugged. 'One of his other bands pulled out at the last minute and he knew you were available.'

'So wait a minute,' said Ad. He had balanced a small stormtrooper helmet on Sebastian's head and was holding him under his arm. 'If we're supporting Marcy Slick, that means we'll be playing big places, yeah?'

I nodded and passed them the itinerary.

'I think I'm going to vom,' said Ad.

Harry took a few thoughtful puffs on his pipe. 'Now, now. This might be an opportunity for us.'

He's actually going for it! said Hank.

'We could go on stage and play like we used to,' Harry went on. 'Then, because we are incredible, PGS will see that they've made a mistake and will let us record an album on our own terms.'

Ad still didn't look convinced, but I was impressed with Harry's idea and already felt less guilty about dragging them into this. Maybe it would work. This plan might actually solve all our problems after all.

'But what about Sebastian?' said Ad. 'He needs the hot tub.'

I imagined our backstage demands.

XPERIENCE RIDER

• Four bottles of water.

• Two pizzas.

• A hot tub for a lobster.

'Jackson says we'll have a tour bus, so you can bring a tank and put it in there,' I said.

'Serious?' said Ad.

'Yeah, of course,' I said.

Ad grinned and lifted Sebastian up to his face. 'Did you

hear that, boy? We're going on our holidays!'

The front door opened and Dad walked in playing his favourite song ('Basic Beeatch') on his phone. ''Sup, homies!'

'All right, K-Dawg,' said Ad, ignoring my order that no one is to call him that under any circumstances. 'We're going on tour!'

Dad stopped the music.

'You're messing with me, yo!'

Oh no. This wasn't how it was supposed to go. This was going to be awkward.

'Nah,' said Ad. 'We're supporting Marcy Slick.'

Dad jumped up and down. 'Marcy Slick is a stone cold FOX. Imma make her forget all about that goat husband of hers.'

'Uh, Dad,' I tried to stop him, but he wasn't listening. He skipped around the flat, striking poses and beatboxing.

'It's gonna be so rinsing, man,' he said. 'Hey, maybe I'll be your groupie guy.'

'Dad . . .'

'You know, scoping the best honeys from the crowd.'

'Dad . . .'

'When do we leave? Will I have time to pick up some new bling?'

'DAD!'

He stopped bouncing. 'What is it, G?'

I took a deep breath and closed my eyes. 'You're not coming on tour.'

Basically, Jackson gave me the choice. We'll have a tour manager so we could either bring the chaperone or not. It took me about three milliseconds to decide.

When I opened my eyes again, a tiny part of me felt guilty. Honestly, Dad looked as if I'd told him he was dying.

'Oh,' he said. 'Yeah, that's cool. Totally cool. I guess I'll just hang here.'

With that, he went into his bedroom.

'Bloody hell, old son, that was brutal,' said Harry.

'Oh come on,' I said. 'Would you rather he comes with us?'

'Good lord, no,' he said.

And they weren't the only people I had to tell. I'd just come straight from Ealing where I broke the news to Mila and Kristoff. They were partway through another keyboard lesson.

'Oh,' Mila said. 'That's really great. It really is.'

Did you hear that, blog? She thinks it's GREAT!

Sunday 9th March

FROM: Joe Cowley
TO: Natalie Tuft
Subject: Big news!

« Older posts

Hi Natalie,

I said I'd keep in touch with everything that's happening, so here we are.

We are going on tour! Not on our own but as a support act. Remember Marcy Slick? Was massively famous, then went mad and there were all those rumours about her weird farm up in the hills? Her! Now you're a motorist, you'll have to drive over to one of the shows.

The plan is to go onstage and play like we used to, give them something real rather than the cack on the album. As well as being the right thing to do, it's the only way we could get Greeny out of his bedroom. He'd been locked in there for twenty-four hours and all we could hear was metal tapping. Very weird.

Anyway, I'm sure we can get you backstage passes. Maybe two, if you want to bring Jed.

Cowley x

FROM: Natalie Tuft
TO: Joe Cowley

Subject: RE: Big news!

Hey Cowley!

Me and Jez will defo try to get to one of them. We're a little tied up at the moment, though. As I write this, I'm sitting in the cab of a lorry heading for Inverness to protest gas drilling. Jez is President of the youth wing of the campaign group, so he's going to make a speech. So proud!

Cheers,

Nat x

PS Yeah, we hitch-hike now. Exciting or what?

Wait a minute, I thought she has her own car.

Tuesday 10th March

Now, I don't know much about fashion, and a quick look in my wardrobe will bear that out, but even I know there was nothing wrong with XPERIENCE's look—old brown coats with their logo on the back—I thought it was kind of cool.

Well, Jackson didn't think so because he booked them in for a morning with Vincente De Barr, apparently the hottest stylist in the country. So now, they look like this:

« Older posts

I mean, look, they even have fake tattoos! Plus, they've made Harry stop using his pipe and Ad take his glasses off. If he doesn't get contacts soon, he's just going to fall off the stage.

Wednesday 11th March

Transcript from an interview with XPERIENCE *on Capital TV—a local station. Jackson gave them the brief: 'Promote the album, promote the tour, and don't say anything stupid.'*

INTERVIEWER
Hello and welcome back to part two of *Music Chat*. I'm here now with up-and-coming dance-pop trio, XPERIENCE.

XPERIENCE
[AWKWARDLY MUMBLE HELLOS]

INTERVIEWER
So, guys, I hear you're in the studio recording your debut

album, LOL. What can we expect from that?

HARRY

Good question, old bean. You can expect music of vary-
ing quality. Some of it bad, some of it awful.

INTERVIEWER

[LAUGHING UNEASILY] And you're about to head out
on tour supporting Marcy Slick. That's got to be a thrill,
right? What are you most looking forward to about that?

AD

Seeing if she's really married to a goat, mainly.

INTERVIEWER

[CLEARING HIS THROAT] Hahahaaaanyway, moving
swiftly on. [QUIETLY TO AD] Are you trying to get us sued?
[LOUDER TO EVERYONE] So, what would you say your
long-term aspirations are?

GREENY

To sack our horrible A & R guy off so we don't have to
look like the gayest football hooligans in the world.

INTERVIEWER

Well, this has been . . . illuminating. XPERIENCE—thanks

« Older posts

for joining us.

AD

Balls. Hee hee. I just swore on telly.

HARRY

[GIGGLING] Arse-puffin.

INTERVIEWER

Can we cut their mics please?

When Jackson got us in the green room afterwards, he was not happy. A vein in his forehead that I had never noticed before was pulsing hypnotically and he chugged some pills straight out of the container without even washing them down with a glass of water.

'You have two reasons to be thankful,' he said. 'One: Capital TV has an audience of about seven people, and two: there is no way I could kill you here and get away with it.'

We all looked at each other. Ad still had a smile on his face after saying 'balls'.

Jackson paced up and down, rubbing his forehead. 'Right, as of now, Harry and Ad, you two are the silent ones. Under no circumstances do you ever speak. Greeny is the voice of the group.'

'But the *SOUND EXPERIENCE* is ours!' said Harry.

Jackson stopped and got in Harry's face. 'Well you should have thought of that before you said "balls" on television.'

Harry cleared his throat. 'Actually, I said "arse-puffin".'

Jackson held a finger up. 'No more talking,' he whispered. 'From now on, no more talking.'

Thursday 12th March

The day before the tour starts. I've got all my stuff packed and ready to go.

I was sitting in the lounge, enjoying the quiet, relishing the prospect of at least three weeks with no Jackson and no Dad. We'd finally be free to do our own thing, to be sophisticated young men.

Then my phone rang.

'Hi, Jackson.'

'Whatever,' he snapped. 'Listen, President Ampleforth has just been on the line. He's bringing me in as joint tour manager.'

I facepalmed. 'Oh.'

'Oh is right,' he said. 'The only reason I'm getting dragged into this is because *XPERIENCE* are supporting. I was planning on heading to Aruba but now I'm going to bloody Cardiff instead. Still, at least I'll be there to personally keep an eye on you. And remember what I said. This fails and it's you who takes the fall.'

Then he hung up.

OK fine. So Jackson being there wasn't ideal, but there was no way he could be with us all the time. This was only a small road bump, I told myself.

That was when Dad emerged from his bedroom with a bag over his shoulder and his decks under his arm.

'Where are you going?' I asked him.

'Leaving,' he said.

'But I thought you were stay-ing here while we're on tour.'

He shook his head. 'Record company told me they've got no use for a chaperone when there's nobody to chaperone.'

I looked away so I didn't have to see his sad puppy face. 'Well, I suppose you should head back to your flat. You've probably got loads of mail to open and stuff.'

Dad sighed as he put the decks down and sat on the sofa. 'There is no flat.'

I looked at him again. 'What do you mean?'

'I moved out,' he said. 'Too many bad memories. I've got nowhere to go.'

Ah Jeez, Hank groaned.

'But surely you knew you couldn't live here forever,' I said. 'You'd have to get your own place eventually.'

Dad nodded sadly. 'You're right, son. I just didn't want to face it yet. See, I'd never lived alone before and it turns out I ain't too good at it. When I found out there was an opportunity to come and live with you, I leapt at it. And it's been one of the best times of my life—getting to be with my boy after only seeing him once a week for so long.'

Cold fingers of guilt wrung out my guts like soggy swimming trunks.

'It might surprise you to find this out, yo,' he went on, 'but your old dad is a very lonely man.'

I didn't know what to say.

'But I guess I've got no choice,' he said, getting back up. 'I'll see you around, son. It's been real.'

He picked his stuff up and headed for the door.

'Dad, wait,' I said.

He stopped and turned around.

'Look, maybe you can come on tour with us after all.'

Who authorized that? Hank screamed.

'Really?' said Dad.

'I suppose so. I'll have to clear it with Jackson first.'

Dad threw his stuff down, picked me up and grabbed me

in a bear hug. 'You're the best, son. I promise you won't regret this.'

I've got a feeling I will.

Friday 13th March

OK, all our stuff is packed and all our paperwork is in order. We are now officially on tour! Forget Dad and Jackson, I will be spending EVERY NIGHT with Mila in fancy hotel rooms with no inflatable lobster hot tubs. I'm so excited I might puke!

6 p.m.

OK, I still think I might puke, but for slightly different reasons.

Jackson called a tour meeting in a big conference room at PGS before we headed out. It was us, roadies, technicians, the backing band, and their assistants, including Mila.

'OK, people,' said Jackson. 'Travel arrangements are as follows—Marcy, her entourage and senior management, including me, stay in the nearest five-star hotel to the venue. Backing band and assistants stay at the nearest four-star, and road crew, nearest two-star. Any questions?'

Me, Dad, Harry, Ad, and Greeny looked at each other. I guessed I was going to have to be the one to speak up.

I put my hand up.

Jackson rolled his eyes. 'What is it, Joe?'

'What about the support act?' I said. 'Do we stay in the nearest one-star hotel?'

Jackson chuckled. 'No, we've got you something even better.'

'It's a camper van,' I said.

He'd taken us out to the loading bay after the meeting to show us our accommodation. I suppose I should have seen it coming.

'I prefer the term "mobile suite",' said Jackson.

'I prefer the term "crap bucket",' said Ad, looking it up and down.

Jackson made a 'zip it' gesture and said, 'No talking, remember?'

I peered in through the window and saw some bunk beds. So Mila was staying in a hotel with Kristoff, and I would be outside, freezing to death and breathing in a disgusting cocktail of everyone's farts.

I took Jackson to one side. 'Look,' I said. 'Technically, I'm management aren't I?'

Jackson shrugged. 'In a manner of speaking.'

'So, you know, shouldn't I be in a hotel? Say, the same one as the backing band? And the assistants?'

Jackson smiled and slapped me on the shoulder. 'But that won't do, will it? I need you here, making sure your guys are behaving.' He leaned in close to my ear. 'Because we know what happens if they don't, don't we?'

He clicked at a woman leaning against the wall, smoking. 'You the driver?'

'Who's askin'?' she said, in the most Scottish accent I've ever heard in my life.

'Your boss is asking—now are you the driver or not?'

The woman threw her cigarette down and stomped over to us. 'You the boss man, are ye?' she said. 'Well, I need a word with you, pal.'

It was weird. Normally 'pal' is a friendly word, but the way she said it made it sound like a deadly threat.

'I'm listening,' said Jackson.

'This van,' she said, pointing at it with two fingers, 'is a heap of shite. I haven't driven anything this bad since Iraq.'

Oh, said Norman. *Do you think she was a soldier?*

Nah, said Hank. *She probably just vacations in war zones. You freakin' moron.*

Jackson laughed as if he couldn't believe what he was hearing. 'I personally selected that vehicle so I know there is nothing wrong with it.'

The driver folded her arms. 'Oh aye, and what do you know about motors?'

'Enough to know that if you don't shut up and drive it, I'll have you down the dole office.'

She got right in Jackson's face, then seemed to think better of it and stepped back. 'You're lucky I need the money.'

Jackson wafted the smoke breath out of his face and turned back to me. 'I'll leave you to it, then. And remember what I said.'

I nodded as he walked away.

The driver stuck her hand out. I shook it and winced as she nearly crushed my hand into dust.

'The name's Mo,' she said.

« Older posts

'What's your band called?'

'Um, XPERIENCE,' I said.

She sniffed. 'Never heard of ye. Doesn't matter, though. I'll get you from A to B in no time. I'm the best driver there is. Three tours of duty in Iraq, three in Afghanistan.'

I nodded. 'Well, I'm sure we won't get blown up then!'

Mo's scowl deepened. 'Don't joke about war, pal,' she whispered. 'War is hell. You understand me?'

I nodded again. I don't think I've ever nodded so much in my life.

Mo grunted, then hocked a load of gozz onto the floor. 'Right,' she said. 'Let's hit the road, ye great fairy.'

12.30 a.m.

There wasn't much travelling involved to the first date tonight. It was at the Gargantua Dome in East London. It was mad, seeing it looming on the horizon. I started to feel a bit sick but I'm not sure whether that was just travel nausea. See, as well as everything else, it turns out Mo isn't what you'd call a laid-back driver—swerving, beeping, and screaming, 'Get oot the way, ye bawbag!' all the way across London. Ad had wedged his tank under his bunk so it couldn't move, but had Sebastian clutched to his chest the entire time anyway. Plus, Greeny had lugged this huge metal chest onto the bus and wouldn't let any of us anywhere near it. Proper freaky.

Jackson was already there to meet us and immediately led us onto the stage. It really was enormous.

'Rinsing, man,' said Dad. 'Hey yo, check this.'

He bounced to the front of the stage and yelled, 'Yo yo yo, London, make some nooooiiissee!'

A bloke cleaning the seats about thirty rows back went, 'Yay!'

'Twelve thousand capacity, boys,' said Jackson. 'Completely sold out.'

Greeny gulped. 'OK, you can shut up now.'

Jackson laughed and gave his shoulders a rough massage. 'Nervous?'

Greeny just nodded. I get why he was feeling like that. I wouldn't have wanted to do it, either.

'Nothing to it, wee man,' said Mo. 'Wait until you're surrounded by a hundred Taliban with only a pistol and a spare pair of drawers, then we'll talk aboot nervous.'

Jackson said, 'Only official XPERIENCE personnel should be on stage. Drivers must wait in their vehicles.'

Mo muttered something about 'slapping the nut' on Jackson and stomped off.

'Right, old boy,' said Harry. 'When's our soundcheck?'

Jackson made a hand signal at the sound booth and they blasted out a snippet of one of their songs before quickly cutting it off. 'There,' he said.

'Wait a minute,' said Harry. 'What's all that about? We're

not playing live?'

Jackson laughed so hard, he nearly cried. 'Yeah, good one. The sound guys are going to play some tracks from the new album and you are going to stand there and look like you're playing them.'

Harry looked is if he was going to pop like an overinflated balloon. 'But that's outrageous!'

Jackson chuckled. 'That's showbiz.'

After that, he led us backstage, where Mo was communicating with some roadies in what sounded to me like a series of grunts.

'Right, now I'm going to show you to your dressing room,' Jackson said. 'But first, I have to tell you the golden rule of this tour.'

Before he could tell us what it was, a tall woman in a shiny tracksuit walked around the corner, surrounded by bodyguards. It had to be Marcy Slick, but she looked proper different to how she does on TV.

Jackson quickly bowed his head and looked at the floor, sending us a non-verbal message to do the same. We all did. Well, most of us.

'Hey,' a voice I think belonged to one of the bodyguards said. 'No eye contact with Ms Slick.'

'I couldn't help it,' said Dad. 'She's looking so fly, it'd be a crime not to admire the view.'

Oh GODDDDD!

'Who is this imbecile?' Marcy hissed.

'This is your support group, Ms Slick,' said Jackson, still looking at the floor. 'I'm sorry for their impudence.'

'They look at me again and they're off the tour,' said Marcy, before leading her entourage down the corridor.

When she was safely out of the way, we looked up again.

'She seems lovely,' said Harry.

'That was the golden rule I was about to tell you about,' said Jackson, before turning on Dad. 'So do me a favour. Never talk to her. You scoring with Marcy Slick is about as likely as that outfit you're wearing ever being fashionable again.'

'So extremely likely, then?' said Dad.

Jackson grumbled something under his breath and opened the door to our dressing room. And by dressing room, I mean cleaner's cupboard. Apparently, we were supposed to have a real one, but it was being used by Marcy as a place to store all her lilies.

I looked at Greeny. He seemed oddly calm for someone who'd just found out they were going to have to mime to terrible songs in front of thousands of people. I asked him if he was OK.

'Course I am,' he said. 'I've just got to head back to the van. I left some stuff in there.' And with that, he left. Dad did too, saying he was going to 'scope the scene for chicas'. Why the hell couldn't I have stayed strong and left him at home?

'This is bloody dire, soldiers,' said Harry, sitting on a barrel of disinfectant. 'Joe, you're our manager, you have to sort this out. Go and speak to Mila, see if she can have a word with some higher-ups or something.'

I pretty much knew it would have no effect, but I wanted to see her so said I'd try. I could hear the strains of a song I vaguely recognized from the radio, so I headed for the stage. Sure enough, the backing band was soundchecking. I found Mila by the side of the stage, watching them.

'Oh, hi, Joe,' she said. 'That's too bad about the van.'

'Hmm,' I mumbled.

'I don't want to rub it in,' she said, 'but I am staying in such a nice hotel room. I got upgraded to a deluxe suite. With a Jacuzzi. A real one, not an inflatable.'

'Ah great,' I said. 'We've been told we have to shower at service stations. I mean, can you imagine the bacteria in a service station shower? And Mo has told us that she will only stop once on every journey and that if we're desperate for the toilet, we have to use the Pringles pipe.' I leaned forward and lowered my voice. 'Number one or number two.'

Mila laughed. 'Well, you're more than welcome to bathe in my tub tonight.'

Wait, what did she just say?

My mouth flapped open and shut and I became unbearably hot. My sophisticated veneer had been decimated, and suddenly I was fourteen again and accidentally calling

Lisa Hall 'Steve'.

'B-but I haven't brought my swimming trunks,' I said.

Norman and Hank looked at each other and sighed. Hank then calmly sat down, put his head in his hands and howled like a wolf.

Mila laughed. 'Oh, I'm sure you'll get by. So what do you think? Van or Jacuzzi?'

'Jjjjjacaaaa,' was the best my brain could do.

It wasn't until I got back to the others that I realized I hadn't mentioned anything about the dressing room. Luckily, that was now the least of their problems. Greeny still hadn't come back, and the closer we got to show time, the more concerned I became.

The pre-show music boomed around the arena. I took a sneaky peek around the curtain and shielded my eyes from the blinding lights. It was about three quarters full.

I looked at the guys. Ad had already filled the cleaner's bucket with puke and Harry was sucking on a drinking straw as a replacement for his pipe.

Jackson appeared next to us like some kind of vampire. 'It's ten minutes to show time. Where's Greeny?' he said.

'I don't know,' I said. 'Maybe he's in the van—I'll go and check.'

'It's all right, everyone,' Greeny's voice came from behind. 'I'm here now.'

I started saying 'Oh, thank God,' but when I turned around and actually saw 'Greeny' it sounded more like 'Gagagagaaaaaaaaaarrrgghh!'

Harry gasped. Jackson turned purple.

The thing that came in was not Greeny. Well, not in the traditional sense. It was a shop mannequin in some of Greeny's clothes, strapped to a motorized stand-up scooter. Greeny's real face stared back at us from an iPad attached to the mannequin's face.

'Greeny, what the hell?' I cried. 'Is this what was in that chest?'

Greeny smiled. 'Did you really think I was going to go on that stage and pretend to sing in front of all those people? This is a compromise. I'm controlling this Greeny substitute from a secret location.'

« Older posts

Jackson grabbed the mannequin's shoulders and got in the iPad's face. 'Listen to me, you little freak. You are going to come out from your hidey-hole immediately or so help me God, I will find you and murder you, do you understand me?'

The Greeny unit turned towards me and said, 'Someone's touchy. Look, it'll be fine. I'll be there on stage without actually having to be there.'

Dad popped his head around the corner from where he was trying unsuccessfully to chat up one of the lighting technicians. 'Just so you know, dudes, if Greeny no-shows, I will step in. I'm sure the boys will vouch for my rhyming skills.'

We all looked at each other. 'I'll go and find him,' I said.

I tried the obvious places first, but had no luck. My brain was racing a jillion miles an hour. If Greeny didn't turn up for this, I would be finished and that knobber Kristoff would be trying to worm his way into Mila's affections/Jacuzzi.

I looked in every room backstage but found no trace of him. I glanced at my watch. Four minutes until show time. He was nowhere in the backstage area so where was he? I was all out of ideas. Except one.

I headed back to the curtain area. Ad was busy playing 'stop hitting yourself' with the Greeny mannequin.

I took out my phone and FaceTimed Scott. I quickly explained the situation to him, then held my phone up to the iPad screen.

My insides churned as I watched Greeny bat away Scott's attempts to talk him around. His every 'you'll be great, babe' was dismissed with a 'no I won't'.

'Listen, old son,' said Harry, 'if Greeny's terrifying robo replacement is inadequate, Ad and I can go out and play live.'

'No way,' said Jackson. 'If he doesn't show, you're all finished.'

The show manager leaned around the corner and said, 'Two minutes to show time.' A single bead of sweat ran the length of my spine.

'Listen,' Scott said. 'Remember how we met?'

Greeny sighed and said, 'Maybe.'

'Yes you do,' he said. 'I found you on Facebook and messaged you after I saw you performing that song at *BUZZFEST.*'

'Yeah, but.'

'But nothing. You did it then and you can do it now. I believe in you.'

Greeny closed his eyes and nodded. 'Fine. I'll do it.'

We all looked at each other as if the governor had sent a last minute pardon right before the warden flicked the switch.

'Of course you will, now go get 'em!'

'One minute to show time.'

« Older posts

I said a quick goodbye to Scott and hung up on him. 'Right, get down here now,' I said to the iPad.

Greeny nodded and got up. He was with us shortly afterwards. Apparently, he'd been hiding in a wardrobe in Marcy's lily room.

Harry pulled him in for a huddle with Ad as the house lights went down and we were plunged into darkness. The crowd whooped and screamed.

Jackson picked up a cordless mic.

'Ladies and gentlemen, boys and girls, welcome to the Gargantua Dome! Please welcome to the stage the hottest thing in dance, XPERIENCE!'

The cheering died down a bit. I guess they'd been hoping Marcy was coming out.

The three of them stood there as if they'd been frozen. They've done big shows before but none this size. I was about to give them some words of encouragement, but before I could, Jackson grabbed Ad by his vest and threw him through the curtain. I looked at the monitor and saw him fall flat on his face, much to the amusement of the thousands of fans. Harry followed and helped Ad up, throwing in a wave to the crowd. Greeny still wouldn't move.

'You'll be fine,' I said to him. 'Do it for Scott, yeah?'

Greeny silently mouthed something that looked like, 'I want to go home.'

A loud track I didn't recognize started up and Jackson grabbed Greeny's shoulder.

'You're the star of the show, Greeny,' he said. 'Probably for the first time in your life, am I right?'

Greeny shrugged.

'I am right,' said Jackson. 'Now get out there and show them you can do it.'

Greeny nodded quickly, as if he was trying to convince himself. 'OK,' he said, and strode through the curtain just in time to mime the opening line.

I watched their set from the monitor. Greeny was surprisingly good. I mean, he really did look like he was singing rather than just moving his lips.

« Older posts

I didn't see Harry and Ad because the cameramen didn't seem that interested in filming them. When they did, it looked like they were just standing there, doing nothing.

Jackson stood next to me, constantly talking to himself. 'That was good . . . need to work on that.' In the end, I asked if there was any way I could go out front and watch. A member of the backstage crew led me to a door, which took me to a little kind of alley in front of the stage reserved for photographers.

I turned around. It was easier to see the crowd from in front of the stage and they seemed fairly into it. Well, some of them did. I did see one bloke, who must have been a dad bringing his daughters to the concert, with massive wads of cotton wool sticking out of his ears. It made me smile because it reminded me of Clifton, Natalie's family's old gardener, who accompanied us to that *BUZZFEST* competition gig. God, that feels like forever ago. I got my phone out and snapped a photo to send to her. I hoped that seeing it would liven up whatever boring political rally Jez had dragged her to.

After the gig, and Jackson had praised Greeny and said nothing about Harry and Ad, we all split up. Harry and Ad went to catering, Dad hung around near the food stands, telling everyone walking past that he was with us, Greeny headed back to the dressing room/cleaner's cupboard to call Scott, and I met Mila on a galley above the side of the stage to watch the Marcy Slick gig. We made sure to get up there well ahead of time so as to avoid any awkward eye-contact situations.

Mila squeezed my hand as the lights in the arena went out and the crowd roared. 'Look at Kristoff,' she said.

I thought, *Ugh, do I have to?*

I peered down at the stage, which was by now bathed in purple light. Kristoff played the opening chords to 'Kiss Me Baby' and the audience went mental.

'He told me he couldn't wait to play that!' Mila yelled over the music. 'He sounds great, doesn't he?'

Luckily, I didn't have to answer because the noise that went up when Marcy Slick appeared on stage in a tight-fitting leather jumpsuit would have drowned it out anyway. Honestly, if the control room were real, Hank and Norman would have come vibrating out of my ears.

The noise didn't let up the entire time we were there. People seemed really happy to see Marcy back and obviously weren't bothered by the goat rumours.

Towards the end of the show, Mila had to go down to get drinks ready for the backing band. I went with her, but Jackson grabbed me and said it was time to head back to the van.

'Why do we have to go now?' I asked. 'The show isn't over yet!'

Jackson led me to the loading area where Harry, Ad, Greeny, Dad, and Mo were already waiting for me. Greeny was signing autographs for a crowd of about twenty people. I saw Harry offer to sign stuff too, but they ignored him.

'You have to be up bright and early tomorrow,' said Jackson. 'You have a full morning of interviews.'

'I get that,' I whispered, 'but I'm not being interviewed, so surely I can stay up a while longer?'

Jackson laughed. 'But you're their manager—you have to be there to make sure the interviews pass without incident.'

I sighed. I guessed I would have to wait on the bus until Jack-

son left and then sneak out to Mila's hotel and her J-Ja-Ja . . . her fancy bath.

I climbed onto the bus and sat by the table. Ad got into his bed and pulled Sebastian out of the tank. Dad dropped his medallion onto the worktop with a loud clank, while Mo got on and sat in a chair in the back. 'Hey, lads,' she said. 'Want to see my war wound?'

None of us knew what to say to that. I think we felt that if we said no, she might actually kill us. Before we could respond, Jackson stuck his head through the door.

'Oi, driver,' he said. 'Get behind the wheel. These lads need to be in Cardiff for five a.m.'

Mo spun around. 'You what, pal?'

Jackson tapped his expensive-looking watch. 'Time is money. I need you out of this car park, pronto.'

Mo grumbled the most disgusting swearwords in the universe under her breath and stomped to the driver's seat.

'It's a good job I don't need sleep,' she said.

Wait! Hank yelled. *No! This cannot happen! Do something, idiot!*

As Mo started pulling the van out of the car park, I made my way to the front.

'Um, Mo?'

'What's up?'

'I was wondering if you could possibly do me a favour?'

« Older posts

'Depends what it is, wee man.' She slammed the brakes on, stuck her head out of the window and politely suggested that a fellow motorist might require an eye test.

I gulped. 'I was wondering if you could drop me off at a hotel.'

She sniffed. 'Can't do it. No unscheduled stops. I have my orders and I must carry them out.'

Who the hell are you, the freakin' Terminator? Hank screamed. *Just drop us off!*

Please calm down, Hank, said Norman.

SHUT YER STINKIN' YAP, NORMAN!

'B-but I thought you didn't like Jackson,' I said.

'I don't,' said Mo. 'But he's my commander and I won't commit insubordination. My sergeant in Afghan was a right bawbag but I'd have marched into hell for him. The stupid bawbag.'

'But please, Mo.'

'No means no!' she yelled.

I quickly scurried to the back before she fired me out of the window.

I tried to call Mila and tell her but it rang out. And that wasn't even the worst thing.

'Look, son,' said Dad, 'that sofa bed is a double! Looks like we're bunk buddies, yo!'

I thought I might cry.

After about an hour, Mila FaceTimed me from the jacuzzi. Yep. From the jacuzzi. I could see her Pink Floyd tattoo poking above the surface of the water and everything.

'Joe, where are you?'

I sighed. 'Jackson has made us leave for Cardiff.'

'Already?' she cried. 'But who's going to be my Jacuzzi friend, now?'

I don't know, but we'd better hope it ain't Kristoff, said Hank.

It was then I realized that the first night of the tour could not have gone any worse.

'Heyyy,' said Dad, leaning over my shoulder. 'Fly looking tub, babe.'

You were saying? said Hank.

Saturday 14th March

We were all pretty exhausted by the time we got to Cardiff FM. It's not easy to sleep in a hard bed in a van driven by a lunatic. Especially when it's with your dad.

Our interview was at six thirty. At six, Jackson texted, telling me to go in with them and ensure that nothing went wrong. I replied and asked why Harry and Ad had to be there if they weren't allowed to speak. He said something about how they must be seen to be a unit at all times. Dad went for breakfast with Mo. I can't imagine what the two of

« Older posts

them can have to talk about.

I sat at the back of the studio while Greeny, Harry, and Ad took the seats opposite the DJ—a bloke called Crazy Jeff.

He started by playing one of the finished songs from LOL called 'I Wanna Be Your L.O.V.E.R.'. When it was over, Crazy Jeff asked them what it was like hearing their music on the radio. Harry responded by blowing a raspberry, which wasn't against the rules because it technically isn't a word. Greeny did his best to answer all the questions himself, but I could tell he was struggling.

I checked my phone. Email from Natalie.

Hi Cowley,

I'm so sorry, but we won't be able to come to the Wolverhampton date. It's the same night we're protesting the new fried chicken place in town. We'll try and hitch to one of the later ones, promise!

Nat x

I wonder if this Jez ever does fun stuff? I mean, can he just chill out and eat a pizza or does he get all worked up about the exploitation of pepperoni?

After that we had a few hours to kill so the others went off to explore Cardiff and I went to Mila's new hotel. When I got there she was in the lobby, drinking coffee alone.

I said hi and leaned in for a kiss, but she shushed me. I followed her eyeline to the corner of the lobby, where Kristoff was playing a piano.

'Isn't it amazing?' Mila whispered. 'It's like having my own private concert.'

Kristoff looked over at her and smiled.

'Incredible,' I said, my face a death mask of fury.

When he finished the song, he stood up and bowed. Mila clapped and whooped. Then he grabbed a flower from a vase and gave it to her.

« Older posts

'Hey, man,' he said to me. 'I watched your boys last night. How come they weren't playing live? Technical hitch?'

'Something like that,' I growled.

'Oh, Joe,' said Mila. 'I'm really sorry but it turns out we won't be able to spend the day together. Marcy has ordered the band in for extra rehearsals and I have to be there.'

'She's a perfectionist,' said Kristoff, taking a seat next to Mila.

If by 'perfection' he meant 'mental' then he was probably right.

'Does she let you make eye contact with her?' I asked.

Kristoff took a sip of his drink and grimaced. 'The way I see it, man, it doesn't matter about eye contact, it's the connection you make with your soul.'

I glanced at Mila to see if she found that as gut-churningly corny as I did, but she looked proper touched.

'OK,' I said. 'Well, we can do something tonight though, right?'

I was determined not to get back in that van. I would run and hide if necessary.

'Actually, we were just talking about that,' said Kristoff.

Oh, I bet you were, you ivory-tickling WUSS! Hank screamed.

'Kristoff has heard about this wonderful Afghan restaurant,' said Mila. 'I've never tried Afghan food before so he said he'd take me. Hey, you should come, too!'

Kristoff looked like someone had gone number one in his flat white. 'Yeah,' he said, proper unenthusiastically. 'That would be great.'

When I got back to the van to head over to the arena, I sat up front with Mo. Harry wanted to sit there to begin with because they had been having an 'intriguing' discussion about the Franco-Prussian War, but I managed to convince him to let me have the spot.

'So, Mo,' I said, in a short gap when she wasn't screaming at pensioners at a zebra crossing to 'get a bloody move on'. 'We're not going to be on the road tonight, are we?'

'Don't think so, wee man,' she said. 'Then again, you never know when that pish talker's going to change his mind. Why?'

'Well, because I kind of have a date tonight,' I said, wondering why I suddenly felt embarrassed. 'You know, with my girlfriend.'

Mo looked at me, and I wished she hadn't because she nearly killed four cyclists. 'You planning on staying out?'

I shrugged. 'Maybe.'

She shook her head. 'Then no can do. A platoon has to stay together.'

God, I can see why Harry likes her so much.

'Please, Mo,' I said. 'If I don't go, that keyboard-playing idiot will be alone with her. Which is EXACTLY what he wants.'

« Older posts

Mo went quiet, then turned down the radio and leaned closer to me. 'You saying another bloke's sniffing round your girl?'

'Well, yeah.'

She seemed to consider this for a second, then nodded. 'Right, pal. I'll make an exception. As long as you promise me one thing.'

'Yeah,' I said. 'Anything.'

'If this lad tries anything dodgy, you slap the nut on him.'

I promised. Anything to get her to agree.

'Good,' she said. 'Cos let me tell you something, strictly between you and me.'

'Um, OK.'

Holy crap, she's going to tell you where the bodies are buried, said Hank.

'I had a fella a few years back,' she said. 'Loved him. His name was Rabbie.'

Ah, so that explains the tattoo on her forearm. I just thought she was really into Jewish holy men.

'I thought he was the one,' she went on. 'But when I got home from Afghanistan, I found out he'd been seeing Jeanie Johnston from the Bricklayer's.'

Mo rubbed her eyes and cleared her throat.

'So, were you angry?' I asked, which has to be the most ridiculous question in the history of the galaxy.

'With him?' Mo replied. 'No. I told him "best of luck to

you". Jeanie even bought me a drink at the bar.'

'Well, it was good there were no hard feelings, I suppose,' I said.

'Oh aye, no hard feelings,' said Mo. 'Until I slapped the nut on her.'

Oh.

'So where are you off to tonight?' she asked. 'Do you want me to come with you and keep an eye on this other lad?'

I laughed. 'No, that's OK. We're going to some Afghan restaurant—his idea.'

Mo nodded. 'I'll say one thing for the Afghans—they know how to put on a meal. You'll enjoy it as long as you don't have a sensitive stomach.'

I gulped. The last time I had a curry, I spent the weekend hunched over the toilet bowl. I guess my system can't cope with something as strong as a chicken korma.

Before I could ask what their mildest Afghan dishes were, Dad distracted us by blasting a rap song out of his speakers and flashing gang signs at a Skoda full of nuns.

Mo tutted. 'Why are the handsome ones always so bloody daft?'

Our dressing room at the Cardiff Arena was even smaller than the first one. This time the second biggest room was being used to house Marcy's new Shetland pony.

We had to stay off the corridors for an hour before show time, too. Marcy was Periscoping her backstage preparations to her millions of followers and it wouldn't do to have us spoiling it.

Their set went pretty much the same. Harry and Ad stood there doing nothing. Greeny got a little better, and actually smiled a couple of times.

After the show, Mila, Kristoff, and me got a cab to the restaurant. I saw Greeny being mobbed again, despite him looking like he wanted them all to go away and leave him alone.

The restaurant was called Kabul, and the interior was all wooden and old-fashioned. Kristoff was like, 'Yeah, this place is real authentic.'

'Oh, so have you been to Afghanistan then, Kristoff?' I asked.

He scowled at me. 'No. Have you?'

'No, but our driver fought in the war there.'

Kristoff's eyes darted around the room. 'Probably best not to talk about that here, dude.'

Mila gave me a thin smile as we were led to the table. I immediately decided that Kristoff was the most annoying person I have ever eaten a meal with, and I include Ad with two broken wrists in that. Kristoff kept flipping through the menu and saying, 'Woooow, this all looks great.' Then, when the waiter came to take our order, he said, 'Tell us about your fair country, my man.'

The waiter scratched his head and said, 'Well, I was born in Swansea so I've never actually been to Afghanistan.'

I had to fake a coughing fit to cover my laughter.

Not that I could afford to be too happy. The menu looked so scary and unfamiliar. Lots of stuff was served in yogurt. Now, I like a Fruit Corner as much as the next man, but it doesn't belong anywhere near chicken. Luckily, I found an English food section and was planning on ordering fish and chips.

But then Kristoff piped up: 'Well, it was a tough decision because this all looks grade A one-hundred-per-cent deel-ish, but I'm going to go with the Sabzi Bourani to start and for the main can I get the Murga Karahi plate?'

'And you, sir?' The waiter looked at me.

All of a sudden, I was struck with shame. How could I order fish and chips? Mila would think I was a small-town English loser afraid to try new things, while the cocking Idiot Abroad over there scoffed pickled otter or whatever the hell it was.

'Yeah, I'll have the same as Kristoff,' I said. 'It sounds great.'

Mila squeezed my arm. 'Are you sure, Joe? When we went out for that curry in Hackney that time, you seemed quite ill.'

'No, I'll be fine,' I said, saying it loud in an effort to

convince myself. 'You've got to try new things, isn't that right, Kristoff?'

Kristoff raised his glass of wine and said, 'Too right, little buddy.'

I raised my lemon and lime and fought the urge to chuck it on him.

The meal was actually pretty nice. I thought that maybe since I moved out of Tammerstone, my stomach had got more cosmopolitan. I just wish my brain had.

'I find Kierkegaard too facile,' said Kristoff, over dessert. 'To me, when you're talking existentialists, there is none better than Sartre.'

Mila nodded and stared at him as if he was giving us the meaning of life.

'What do you reckon, Joe?' he said.

'Gah?'

'Existentialists—who's your favourite?'

We've got nothing, said Norman, frantically scanning the database. *NOTHING!*

Listen, kid, you're going to have to create a diversion to get out of this, said Hank. *Smash a plate. Afghans love that kind of stuff.*

That's Greeks, said Norman.

See? We don't know anything! said Hank.

I cleared my throat and prayed to Lord Jebus himself for one of the waiters to come over.

'Um . . . yeah,' I said. 'Like you said . . . Sartre. He's the big dog.'

'Fascinating,' said Kristoff, leaning forward and steepling his fingers. 'So which of his books do you like?'

He smirked across the table as if to say, 'I've got you now.'

Mila looked at me expectantly—her grey manga eyes wide.

'Well, you know,' I said. 'They're all so good, it's hard to pick one.'

Kristoff's smile got wider. 'But if you had to.'

I swear to God, if I were real I would KICK HIS ASS! Hank screamed.

'H . . . his early work?' I said.

I could tell Kristoff was going to press it further, but luckily Mila interrupted and started talking about some other writer I've never heard of.

After dinner, we walked back to the hotel. All the way there, Kristoff was droning on about how he would love to learn Welsh and that it looks like a beautiful language. I said it kind of sounds like Klingon, but he told me off for being 'culturally insensitive' because he's a STUPID IDIOT MORON MORON MORON.

When we got to Mila's room, he gave her a goodnight hug which seemed to go on for too long. Ten full seconds. He's just lucky I'm too civilized to follow Mo's advice of

« Older posts

'slapping the nut on him'.

Once Kristoff had finally Pistoff to his own room to read Fartre and twiddle his daft little beard, I realized what was happening.

We were finally alone.

'So . . .' said Mila.

'So . . .' I replied.

Mila opened the door with her card and we walked inside. The room was super posh, but I could barely take anything in. My head was spinning. My guts were churning.

Mila touched my face and kissed me.

'I really like you, Joe,' she said.

'I really like you, too.'

There was total silence. This was bad news because where there's silence, my brain has to fill it, and the results are never positive. Luckily, Mila took the initiative.

She led me by the hand to a sofa near the balcony. We sat down and started kissing. I mean properly *kissing*.

I was excited and super nervous so the churning in my guts got worse.

And worse.

'Joe, are you OK?'

I was bent double, clutching my gut.

'Mmm hmm, fine,' I said, in a voice that sounded like I was being strangled by an angry chimp.

'Then why are you holding your stomach?' Mila asked.

'No reason.' As soon as I said it, I felt a rushing sensation in my intestines.

'IjusthavetogotothetoiletsorrythankyouI'llbebackinjusta-moment,' I spluttered as I sprinted to the bathroom.

I didn't even have the chance to put the light on. I sat down just in time and quickly flipped on the tap to try to drown out the noise of the grim bum exodus.

You don't need me to get more graphic than that, do you, blog? I mean, for the love of all that is holy, I have never experienced anything like it. I felt like I had been totally emptied.

A quick scan suggests the starter is to blame, said Norman. *Hopefully, that will be it for now.*

As soon as he'd said it, another tsunami happened. Oh God, my eyes were watering. Why the hell did that idiot make us go to an Afghan restaurant? I hope he pukes up his coccyx.

KNOCK KNOCK KNOCK.

« Older posts

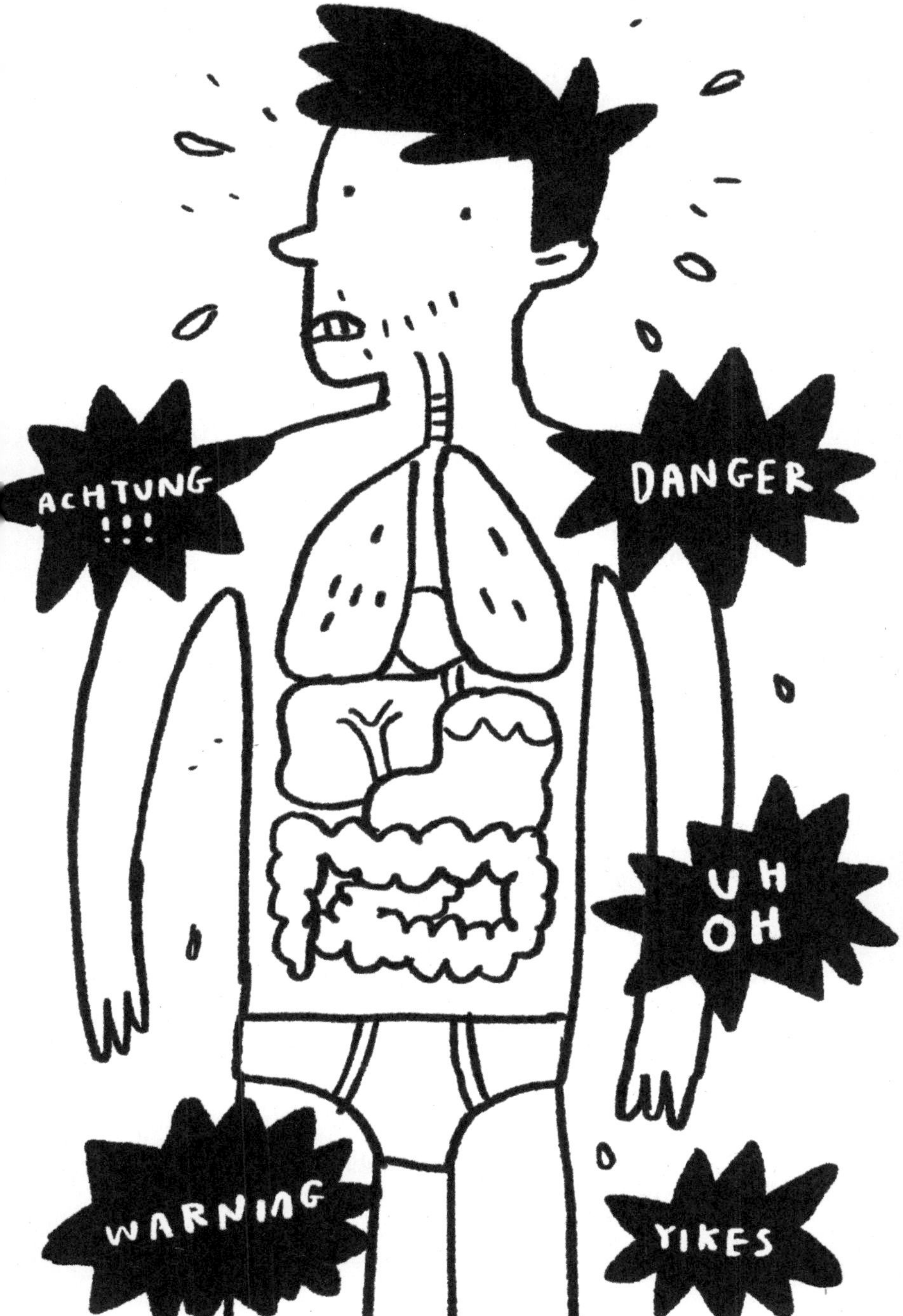
ACHTUNG
!!!
DANGER
UH
OH
WARNING
YIKES

'Joe, are you OK?'

Sweat poured down my face and stung my eyes.

'I'm fine,' I whimpered. 'Just freshening up.'

'. . . In the dark?'

'Yep!' I squeaked.

'I'll just switch the light on for you,' said Mila.

The lights flicked on. Why are hotel bathroom light switches never inside the actual room?

I looked to my right and saw another toilet. *Wow,* I thought. *This must be a really fancy place if the bathrooms have two bogs. Wait a minute.*

I looked down.

What I was sitting on wasn't a toilet at all.

It was a bidet.

Norman frantically tried to formulate some kind of solution, while Hank jumped to his feet and pounded the console.

When a girl asks you back to her place, be charming, drink coffee, tell her how nice she looks, he yelled. *DO NOT DROP A DEUCE IN HER GODDAMN BIDET!*

The only merciful thing about this whole situation was that there was nothing solid enough to get stuck in the plug hole. The smell, though, was unholy. I quickly turned on the tap to wash away the foul-smelling sludge and then sprayed a load of deodorant and perfume around. Then I grabbed a tiny bottle of shower gel and squirted it all around

« Older posts

the basin, before washing that away.

'Joe, are you sure everything's OK?' Mila yelled.

'Everything's fine!' I said. 'Still freshening!'

Christ! Can you smell it in there? Hank screamed. *The only thing that would freshen this is an exorcism.*

Once I'd cleaned up (both myself and the bathroom) and sprayed more body spray, I finally emerged. Mila was sitting on her bed. She patted the space next to her and said, 'Now where were we?'

I responded by nearly crapping my pants and having to run back to the toilet.

You IDIOT! Hank screamed. *You couldn't just have the freakin' fish, could you? No, you HAD to impress her and eat the kooky Middle Eastern stuff. Well, I'm sure she's real impressed now. She is in there, all 'Where were we, lover boy?' and all you can do is violently crap yourself. Well bra-freakin'-vo. That's it, I'm smashing my way out of here and going in there myself.*

There was another knock at the door.

'Joe, do you have a bad stomach?'

I cleared my throat. 'Something like that.'

I thought I could hear a sigh. 'OK. Would you like me to get you anything?'

'N-no thanks,' I said, wondering if I was shivering because I was cold or because I was dying. 'I'll be right out.'

When I finally emerged an hour later, Mila was fast asleep. I climbed in next to her and slept, too.

For about ten minutes before I had to run to the bath-room again.

I wonder if there's a chapter about this in *The Art of Love?*

Sunday 15th March

When I got back in the van the next morning, everyone was staring at me.

'What?' I said.

'So?' said Greeny.

'So what?'

'You know,' said Harry. 'How did it go? How many times did you disappoint her?'

Ad laughed so much, he nearly dropped Sebastian.

I flopped down on my bed. 'How do you know I was with Mila? I could have been anywhere. Besides, it's none of your business.'

You would have thought that would have deterred them.

« Older posts

It didn't.

'None of our business, eh?' said Harry. 'That means things really went wrong. Come on, spill it. Did you call her boobs "lady pillows"?'

'Did you get a nosebleed?' said Greeny.

'Did you call her Natalie?' said Ad.

'No!' I said. 'Why would you think I'd do that?'

Ad shrugged and tried not to laugh. Then they all sat there staring at me, silently moving closer until they sur- rounded me.

'Fine,' I said. 'If I tell you, will you leave me alone?'

'Certainly, old boy,' said Harry.

'OK.' I sat up and looked at them, at least thankful that Dad and Mo were out.

'We went out to dinner at an Afghan restaurant last night and I must have eaten something dodgy because it gave me the runs.'

There was silence for a few seconds. Harry slowly looked at Ad. Ad slowly looked at Greeny. Greeny slowly looked at Harry. Then they instantly started crying with laughter.

'Oh my God,' Harry yelled through shrieks of laughter. 'I knew there was a threat of dirty bombs coming out of Afghanistan, but I didn't think you'd be the one bringing them!'

And it just carried on. When Dad and Mo finally got back and we started our journey, I went and sat at the front. As soon as I did, Mo turned to me, shaking with laughter.

'If you want to stop, pal, let me know,' she said. 'I'm not having you pebble-dashing all over my bloody van.'

Stupid idiots can't keep a secret.

The tidal surges in my guts came and went all day. I kept texting Mila to apologize but she said it was no big deal and that we could meet up again tonight.

When we arrived at the Manchester Times Arena, I was taking small sips of warm water and grimacing. When someone whacked me on the back, I very nearly had another accident.

'Hey, man, I hear you're feeling kinda delicate.'

I growled the worst swear word I could think of under my breath and turned to face Kristoff.

« Older posts

'Something like that,' I said.

He smirked like some massive lopsided arse-face and said, 'Yeah, if you're not too well travelled, Afghan food can be hard on the system.'

'Shows what you know, Christopher,' I said. 'I have actually travelled across Europe.'

Does Birmingham to Benidorm count as 'across Europe'?

Kristoff laughed and patted my shoulder a bit too hard for my liking. 'So Mila tells me you guys met at the *BUZZFEST* I played at. Very cool. Although, if I'd have seen her first, things might have turned out differently.'

He winked at me and strutted off down the corridor, laughing while rage surged through my body.

Actually, said Norman, hanging onto a console to steady himself amid the rumbling, *I think that might be more than just rage.*

Oh no. Not again. This was desperate. If my previous episodes were anything to go by, I had exactly twenty seconds to find a toilet. I was like a volcano, ready to blow. A really disgusting volcano.

Mount Vespoovius! Hank yelled. *High five!*

THAT MIGHT BE MORE THAN JUST RAGE.

HIGH FIVE!

I ran down the corridor, desperately searching for a bathroom of any description. I couldn't go in XPΣRIΣNCΣ's dressing room because it didn't have a toilet, what with it being a disused larder, and the communal one on the corridor was out of order.

Nineteen . . . eighteen . . .

I tried a door. Locked. I tried another. A cleaner's cupboard.

Fifteen . . . fourteen . . .

No. This could not be happening. There had to be another toilet somewhere!

Ten . . . nine . . .

I had tried every door I could find. Except one.

MARCY SLICK. DO NOT DISTURB UNDER ANY CIRCUMSTANCES.

I knew I shouldn't have, but I had no choice. I tried the door and found it open. There was no way Marcy would have been at the arena this early, so there had to be a window of opportunity.

I sprinted past the endless piles of flowers, straight into the en suite. Again, it was a photo finish.

Once the initial panic was over, it was quite pleasant. There was a bowl of rose petals next to the sink and classical music drifted in through some speakers. It was loud enough for me to appreciate it but quiet enough for me to hear MARCY SLICK WALKING INTO HER DRESSING

ROOM.

I jumped up off the toilet and scrambled to the door. The lock-less door.

'OK, Slickys, this is my humble dressing room. I like to chill out here before a show and get into the zone. As you can see, it has a couch, a full-length mirror, and of course, an en suite bathroom.'

NOOOOOOOOOO!

The door opened, and there was Marcy Slick, iPhone in hand, Periscoping me to her millions of followers with my trousers around my ankles and my hands cupped over my privates. She quickly spun around, told her followers she would be back later and closed her phone. By the time she turned around again, I was still scrabbling to pull my kecks up. Stupid shaky hands.

'Who the hell are you and what are you doing in my TOILET?' she barked.

'Um, I'm J-Joe Cowley and I'm really sorry but yours was the only toilet I could find and it was an emergency.'

By the time I'd stammered my way to the end of that sentence, I had finally pulled my trousers up. I thought it would be best to just stare at the floor, partly because of the no-eye-contact rule and partly because I hoped if I stared for long enough, I could magically transport myself to a parallel dimension where I'm not such a cocking idiot.

'Look at me!' Marcy boomed.

'Um, are you sure?'

'DO IT!'

I did as I was told and saw the very same Marcy Slick that I saw wearing a bikini in that music video when I was twelve that made me feel all weird. Except she looked a little bit older and a LOT more furious.

'I remember you now,' she said. 'You're with that crap support band, aren't you?'

Even though I was allowed to make eye contact, I didn't want to, and decided to focus on a watercolour portrait of her on the wall.

'Y-yes, Ms Slick.'

'I thought so,' she said. 'You've already pissed me off once, but this is the final straw. You're sacked. The lot of you.'

« Older posts

No. This could not happen. I could not be the reason for XPERIENCE being kicked off the tour. I would definitely be sacked by Jackson and I would go back to Tammerstone a massive stinking failure.

'Please, Ms Slick,' I said. 'I'm begging you, don't sack us. We're having a rough time because Jackson McHugh changed everything about us and makes us travel in a horrible camper with a driver who might be a psychopath and my annoying hip-hop dad and a lobster called Sebastian and our singer can't sing and tried to stick an iPad to a dummy's face as a replacement and my girlfriend works for your backing band and the keyboard player thinks he's some kind of big shot and I'm pretty sure he wants to steal her from me and I think he might do it because he can play a musical instrument and has travelled and can speak Dutch and he made us go out for Afghan food and my stomach couldn't take it and I've been trying really, really hard to be any good in this business but everything I do is a disaster and I just want to show everyone that I'm not a complete screw-up and please don't sack us.'

By the time I'd finished talking, I had tears in my eyes and my mouth was as dry as a desert. Marcy stared at me for what felt like nine millennia before saying, 'Sit.'

I did as I was told. She sat on the couch and cracked open a bottle of mineral water.

'This is a tough business,' she said. 'Do you really think

you have what it takes?'

I nodded proper hard. 'Yes. Definitely. I definitely do. Definitely.'

Marcy raised a perfectly manicured eyebrow at me.

'OK, maybe not,' I said. 'But I want to get better.'

Marcy lowered her eyebrow and leaned forward. 'I was like you when I started. I was scared stiff that I would never make it—and that fear made me fail. Once I got over that, I could finally succeed.'

I thought about it. Maybe she was right. Maybe I just need to let go of feeling so nervous about everything. Next time Kristoff implies that I don't know something, I should just own it: 'NO, I HAVE NO IDEA WHO KIERKEGAARD IS—HE SOUNDS LIKE A CRAPPY ALIEN FROM BAT-TLESTAR GA-COCKING-LACTICA.'

'Those other boys in the band,' she went on. 'Are they your friends?'

I nodded.

'Prepare for that to change,' she said.

'What do you mean?'

She took a sip of water. 'You don't keep friends in this business. Everyone you know will eventually betray you.'

'Really?' I asked.

She nodded. 'When I had my breakdown, my best friend sold stories about me to newspapers.'

There's no way I could imagine any of the guys doing

that to me. And I know I would never do that to them. I mean, what do I even have on them anyway?

'I-if you don't mind me asking, Ms Slick,' I said, trying to disguise the fact that my entire body was trembling. 'Did the music industry cause your breakdown?'

Marcy looked thoughtful for a second. 'I think it did. I was under pressure to tour again after I had only just got off the road, I had paparazzi hassling me everywhere I went, and I was never out of the gossip columns. It got too much. Even now they still print lies about me. I mean, can you believe people think I married a goat?'

'You mean you didn't?' I said.

'No,' she snapped. 'Yes, I was photographed with a goat in a tuxedo, but what they didn't show you was the sheep in a wedding dress.'

It went quiet for a few seconds.

'So, you were having a wedding for a goat and a sheep?' I asked.

'I was in a very dark place,' she said.

I didn't know what else to say. I couldn't believe I was sitting there having a conversation with Marcy Slick.

'Right, Joe,' she said. 'I've changed my mind—you're not off the tour.'

I sighed with relief. 'Thank you, Ms Slick.'

'But if I ever catch you using my toilet again, you will be,' she said. 'Now, get out.'

I stood up and wobbled my way over to the door like a partially sentient jelly. 'Yes, Ms Slick, thank you, Ms Slick.'

'One more thing,' she said, before I could leave.

'Yes?'

'Go and enjoy being friends with those other guys,' she said. 'While you still can.'

I mean, that can't be right, can it? She's obviously still a bit crazy, and doesn't know what she's saying. Plus, she doesn't really know us.

Yeah, everything's going to be fine.

3 a.m.

When I returned to the larder/dressing room, I discovered that the others had already found the Periscope of me being discovered in Marcy's toilet and had been playing it on a loop.

'What I want to know is, why were your trousers down?' Harry asked after the fiftieth run through.

'I was pooing,' I said. 'You know I was pooing.'

'Course you were, pervert,' said Greeny.

About an hour before show time, Jackson appeared and

whisked Greeny away for a top secret meeting. Greeny didn't seem to know what it was about but went along anyway. It was five minutes before show time when they finally got back.

'What was that about?' Harry asked him.

Greeny looked weird. Like jumpy and odd. 'Nothing,' he said, sneaking a quick glance at a smirking Jackson. 'Just a run-through of the performance.'

Harry and Ad didn't look convinced, but they had to let it go. Once they'd gone on stage, I asked Jackson what their meeting was about. He responded by tapping the side of his nose and saying, 'That's on a need-to-know basis, my friend.'

I checked my phone. Email from Natalie.

Wow, Cowley. Thanks to Periscope, I think I've now seen way more of you than I ever did when we were going out.

Soz again I can't be there tomorrow night.

Nat x

The show was the same as it was the previous two nights—Greeny seemed to be trying a little harder on stage, but they still didn't exactly look comfortable. Harry and Ad just stood at the back again, occasionally pretending to press some buttons on their equipment. I mean, it's all so pointless—they might as well be doing crosswords up there.

I ran into Mila on the corridor. She looked super rushed.

'Sorry I haven't had a chance to meet you tonight,' she said. 'The band are keeping me so busy. We'll meet at my hotel later, OK? That is if you're feeling better?'

I gulped. 'Yes,' I said. 'Loads.'

The backing band's door opened and that moron Kristoff stuck his head out.

'Hey, Mila,' he said. 'I'm having a little shoulder trouble—could you give me a quick rub down?'

Mila smiled and rolled her eyes at me. 'Be right there.'

She gave me a quick kiss and disappeared into the room. Kristoff stayed leaning out and gave me a wink.

'She has the magic touch,' he said, before going in and closing the door.

One of these days, my foot is going to 'magically touch' him right in the balls.

I was about to make my way to Mila's hotel after the show when Jackson caught up with us.

'I need you all in the van,' he said. 'You've got an early morning appearance in Birmingham.'

'What?' I cried. 'Another one?'

« Older posts

'Hey,' he snapped. 'Do you want to promote your album or not?'

'Not especially, old bean,' said Harry.

Jackson gave him the stink-eye and said, 'No talking, remember?'

I couldn't believe what I was hearing.

'Actually,' Jackson went on, 'it's not me you should thank for this big opportunity. It was that lad from Marcy's band.'

Scalding waves of fury burned through my brain. 'Was it the keyboard player by any chance?'

'Yeah, that's the one,' said Jackson. 'He used to be in this band who would regularly go on the *Midlands Morning Show* when they were touring over here. He called in a favour with the producer. Pretty impressive, eh?'

Oh my actual God. He went to these lengths to get me out of the picture? What a scumbag. I wanted to go and find him, but Jackson blocked my way. When Mo found out she was pulling another all-nighter, she got in Jackson's face and demanded a pay rise. Jackson peeled some notes off a wodge he pulled out of his pocket and threw them on the floor before strutting away.

Mo's face was a picture of fury. 'If that man thinks I'm going to demean myself by scrabbling around on the floor for money, he doesn't know Mo McDonald.' She turned to us. 'Ad, pal. Pick up this cash for me, will you?'

On the bus, I called Mila and told her what happened.

And I didn't get off the phone. Every time she went to end the conversation, I would start a new subject. I saw Harry clamp his pillow over his ears, but I didn't care. As long as I was talking to her, I knew that crusty idiot couldn't be doing anything he shouldn't. I even heard him show up at her hotel room. I mean, can you believe that? I would have hijacked the van and turned it around if I wasn't so sure Mo would snap my head off.

Mila told Kristoff she was on the phone to me and would be heading to bed soon. He hung around for a while, trying to weasel his way in, but Mila was having none of it, and I'm sure that would have been the same if she hadn't been on the phone to me.

I'm sure of it.

Monday 16th March

This is my reality now. Waking up when it's still dark on a rock hard bed, listening to a combination of the van's engine grumbling, Dad mumbling Marcy's name down my ear in his sleep, Ad and Greeny rowing because Ad used the sink to bathe Sebastian, and Mo and Harry debating the effectiveness of Churchill as a military strategist.

I shouldn't be here, I should be in a comfortable hotel room with Mila—that was the plan. Tonight, it's happening. I don't care what crappy TV shows (and it is crappy—it's on Sky channel 868) Kristoff pulls out of his arse, I'll get

« Older posts

out of it.

Tonight's gig is at the Wolverhampton Arena. I met up with Mila at the hotel beforehand. I was hoping to find Kristoff to tell him to lay off, but he was nowhere to be found. Besides, Mila was keen to get out because we only had an hour to see the sights of Wolverhampton.

Twenty minutes later, we had seen them.

When I got back to the van, the tension from last night was back. Greeny was still refusing to tell them what that meeting with Jackson was about—saying he had been sworn to secrecy.

'That's it,' said Harry. 'I'm sick of this. Verity's father is the Vice President of PGS's European operation—she can have a word with him and go over Jackson's head. It's not right that we're being forced to live in such squalid conditions.'

I think a combination of the secret meeting and Greeny being mobbed by fans every night was taking its toll on Harry.

He got out his iPad and called Verity on Skype. We all gathered around. She popped up on-screen in a bedroom.

'Hello, my dear,' said Harry. 'Are you free to talk?'

'For about five minutes,' she replied. 'We're heading to the Louvre soon.'

'Hey, speaking of the Louvre, Joe was caught with his pants down in Marcy Slick's!' said Ad.

Verity rolled her eyes. 'It's an art gallery.'

'Yeah, but when Joe was in it, it was a fart gallery,' said Ad.

Harry shot him a look. 'Do you mind?'

Ad backed off, sheepishly. Harry doesn't normally snap at Ad like that.

'We have serious business,' said Harry. 'We believe we are being mismanaged by Jackson McHugh, and—'

He was cut off by Jasmeen running in, wearing only a towel. A muscular bloke in shorts was chasing her.

'Leave me alone, Joshua,' she yelled. 'I'm all wet.'

Verity cleared her throat. 'Um, it's Ad and Harry.'

Jasmeen suddenly went all serious and sat down next to Verity. 'Joshua' followed.

'Wassup, dudes?' he said, in an accent so Australian, it probably wears a corked hat. He had his hand over Jasmeen's bare shoulder. He had to be one of the 'boys' they were talking about.

'Um, I don't believe we've been introduced,' said Harry.

'This idiot is our mate Joshua,' said Verity. 'We met him in Florence and haven't been able to get rid of him.'

'You cheeky little Sheila,' Joshua said as he reached

over and tickled Verity. She screamed with laughter.

The door behind them opened and an even more mus-cular guy emerged. 'Can I hear a tickle fight?' he said.

'Yeah,' Joshua yelled. 'I've got one of them taken care of, so you start on the other.'

The super-buff dude ran at Jasmeen and started tickling her. She looked like she was making a very unconvincing show of trying to stop him.

'Um, excuse me?' said Harry.

He exchanged a glance with Ad as the tickling contin-ued.

'EXCUSE ME!'

They stopped and looked at the camera. The two girls were breathless. Jasmeen even had hiccups.

'I need to speak to my girlfriend,' said Harry.

'Go on then,' said the super-buff one. 'She's sitting right next to you, isn't she?'

Joshua laughed and exchanged a high five with him. 'Good one, mate.'

'You are so BAD,' said Verity, laughing. 'Go on, get out of here, both of you.'

The two 'dudes' left, high-fiving the whole way.

'What a pair of arses,' I said.

'What was that, Joe?' said Verity.

'I said, "What a pair of Aussies."'

'Nice save,' Greeny muttered.

'Anyway, what's up?' Jasmeen asked while fashioning one of those complicated girl turbans.

Harry huffed. 'We are reaching the end of our teth—'

He was cut off again, this time by the two Bruces running in, picking the girls up and carrying them out of the room, screaming.

I looked at Harry. His jaw was clenching and, unless I was very much mistaken, his chin was wobbling.

'Are you OK, Harry?'

Harry shook his head quickly and blew out. 'Of course I am. Now leave me alone, the lot of you.'

We kind of sat around awkwardly and looked away. I mean, when you're in a camper van, where are you going to go?

3.30 a.m.

I can't actually remember the last time I slept through the night. I feel weird. Confused. Different. I don't know how I feel, really.

Just before the show, Jackson came to our cupboard and started coaching Greeny: 'Interact with the crowd more, blah, blah, blah.'

Ad asked if he had any pointers for him and Harry, but Jackson was just like, 'Nah, you're good,' without even looking up. Not that Harry would have been up for that. Since that call to Verity, he had been in a miserable mood.

« Older posts

I was standing in the corridor, trying to get hold of Mila on my phone, when a door opened behind me.

'Psst . . . toilet boy.'

I turned around and there was Marcy Slick, in the green leather catsuit she wears for her opening song.

'Um, hi, Ms Slick,' I said, quickly fixing my gaze on the floor.

'Enough with the no-eye-contact thing,' she said. 'I've seen you half-naked—we're past that now.'

I looked her in the eye even though she scares the hell out of me.

'I've seen Jackson sniffing around your singer,' she said. 'Watch him.'

'Why?' I said. 'What would he be doing?'

'I used to be in a girl band,' she said. 'We never made it big, but we supported bigger artists on tour a few times. Jackson was a junior A & R man back then and it was him who convinced me to leave and go solo. I bet he's trying to do the same thing to you.'

'Seriously? Greeny?'

She nodded. 'I reckon he sees the other two as dead weight. With only one he can make even more money. Take it from me. My first album paid for his yacht.'

After XPERIENCE came off stage, looking like they'd just completed a sixteen-hour shift wiping tramps' arses rather than performing in front of thousands, I intercepted them. I had to find out what was happening before Jackson caught up with them.

'Greeny,' I said, 'these meetings with Jackson—are they about you going solo?'

'About him going WHAT?' Harry yelled.

Greeny's mouth dropped open and his eyes darted around like crazy. 'I don't know what you're talking about.'

Harry and Ad turned around and faced Greeny. 'You're just the special effects man, not Justin bloody Bieber!' Harry yelled.

I tried to get him to calm down, but he was having none of it.

'Honestly, lads,' said Greeny, 'he's just talking to me

about performance things, that's all.'

'POPPYCOCK!' Harry yelled. 'This makes total sense now. It explains all the secrecy.'

Jackson appeared around the corner.

'I couldn't help but overhear,' he said. 'Greeny, you don't have to answer any of their questions, but you guys should know that it's nothing to worry about. The tour is going well. Anyway, you should rest up for a while—you have two magazine interviews before you can leave tonight, then you have another breakfast interview in Leeds first thing tomorrow morning.'

'Hold on a minute,' I said. 'Did Kristoff set this up, too?'

Jackson chuckled. 'Yep. That lad's proving to be quite an asset.'

'Quite an ass-hat, more like,' I said.

There was no way I was getting in that van—not with all the arguing. I hung back and checked the train timetables and figured that if I got a really early morning service, I could be in Leeds for the interview.

I texted Mila and told her I would be able to see her tonight. She replied with loads of kisses and my stomach went all flippy.

By the time we got done with the interviews (super miserable experiences), the show had been over for a while. Mila dropped me another text to say that I should meet her at her hotel room.

When I got outside the arena, it was bucketing it down. I stuck up my hood and headed past the stragglers at the stage door waiting for an autograph from Marcy. Yeah, good luck with that.

According to my maps app, the hotel was a five-minute walk away. I decided to jog and see if I could make it there in two. I'd told the others that I would meet them in Leeds tomorrow morning because I was seeing Mila, but all they said was 'OK.' No jokes about me crapping myself, or having a micropenis. Just OK.

I had reached the street the hotel was on—I could even see it all lit up in the distance—when my phone rang. I was expecting it to be Harry, suddenly remembering that he'd forgotten to take the piss out of me and was ringing to put things right. It wasn't.

'What's up, Gav?'

'Mate, I'm sorry to ring you when you're on tour, but I didn't know what else to do.'

Oh God. What was wrong? Was Mum ill? Something up with the twins? Had Doris carked it?

'It's Natalie.'

Holy crap. I stood under the canopy of a cinema and stuck my finger in my other ear to drown out the noise of the traffic.

'What's happened?'

'I was in that new chicken place with Poppy,' Gav said.

« Older posts

'Jez and Nat were trying to protest it or something like that and they were arguing. Proper nasty. It looked like he was dumping her. She's in a really bad way. Me and Poppy have tried talking to her, but she's having none of it. I thought maybe she could talk to you?'

JEZ has dumped NATALIE? What a moron! How the hell could he do such a thing? Doesn't he know she's the greatest thing that will ever happen to him?

'Yeah, put her on,' I said.

I heard the sounds of the cafe drift through the speakers as Gav walked around. 'Ah man, she's gone.'

'What do you mean?'

'She was here a minute ago, I swear.'

I rubbed my forehead. 'This isn't good. I'm going to have to do something.'

'What?' said Gav.

'Something,' I said again, and hung up.

Without thinking, I ran in the opposite direction of the hotel, towards the train station. I called Natalie on the way. Straight to voicemail. That decided it. When I got to the station, the last train to Tammerstone was about to leave. I quickly jumped on without buying a ticket. There were only two stops, and I would be there within the hour.

My phone went off. Maybe it was Natalie calling me back. I answered quickly.

'Where are you, Joe? I'm waiting.'

Oh balls. Mila. As bad as it sounds, I hadn't even thought about her. In an instant of panic, I had forgotten about our night, and I had forgotten about Kristoff.

'I'm really sorry,' I said. 'I've had to go home. There's been a . . . um . . . family emergency.'

'Oh no!' said Mila. 'I hope it's nothing too serious.'

Guilt twisted my stomach. 'It'll be fine. I'll see you tomorrow.'

When I arrived in Tammerstone, I headed straight to the park. It seems to be the place everyone goes when they're sad about stuff. I remember I found Ad there the day he discovered that the tooth fairy wasn't real. It totally ruined his fourteenth birthday party.

There was no sign of Natalie, though. My panic shifted up a gear. Gav said she was in a bad way. What if she had done something stupid?

From there, I went down to her house. Her bedroom light was off. Maybe she had gone to bed. I tried calling again. Nothing. I thought about knocking on the door, but I guessed I wouldn't exactly be a welcome presence on the doorstep at midnight.

I thought back to when I was banned from her house before. I picked up a pebble from the gravel next to one of the hedge animals and lobbed it at the window. To my amazement, it hit. She didn't come to the window. I tried another. Nothing. She couldn't have been in there. There

« Older posts

was only one other place I could think of.

I crawled through the gap in the fence that led to the school field and ran across it, towards the main building. When I got to the bench and saw Natalie, lit by the orange lamp above her, my heart nearly hopped out of my throat.

'Cowley?' she said. 'What are you doing here?'

'What a welcome,' I said.

She laughed, then immediately burst into tears. I sat down next to her and put my arm around her. She leaned her head on my shoulder and sobbed. I didn't know what to say, so I just let her get it out of her system. Hearing her cry like that was horrible.

'I'm sorry,' I said, when the sobs slowed down.

'No, I am,' said Natalie. 'I can't believe you came off your tour to come and see me. You didn't miss anything important, did you?'

I sighed, thinking about Mila and that idiot Kristoff being in the same hotel. 'It doesn't matter.'

We didn't speak for a while. I just stroked her hair and listened to her jerky breaths.

'Do you . . . want to talk about it?' I asked.

Natalie sat up and rubbed her eyes with the sleeve of her hoody.

'Jez told me he thought we should end things,' she said. 'Apparently, we don't have enough in common.'

I nodded, still not knowing what to say.

'He was right,' she went on. 'We don't. I mean, you have NO idea how many times I took my car out at night for a burger. This once, he found a Big Mac wrapper in my bedroom and I blamed my brother! I mean, Charlie? That kid never eats McDonald's—he reckons they're "nutritionally unviable".'

I laughed, then stopped myself. It didn't seem right. Natalie noticed and laughed, too—a short, bitter, tear-streaked laugh.

'Plus, he made me feel so guilty all the time,' she said. 'I mean, my hair dye. He kept going on about the "catastrophic effect on marine life". It was like dying my hair purple was the same thing as personally murdering Nemo's mum. And I went on all those bloody protests with him, hitch-hiking to get to them. Do you have any idea of the kind of people who pick up hitch-hikers? Weird, lonely people, that's who.' She stopped and sighed.

« Older posts

'So why the hell do I feel like I'm never going to get over it?'

You know what's shameful, blog? While trying to comfort her, I couldn't help but wonder if she'd been this upset about me. What a knob.

'Well, to be honest, Natalie,' I said, trying to put the thought out of my head, 'if he controlled you like that, it's probably a good thing that you've split up. Although I know it probably doesn't feel like it right now.'

Natalie rubbed her cheeks again. 'You're right,' she said. 'I think I just let him get away with it because he's so beautiful.'

'Could have done without hearing that,' I mumbled.

'Looking back, I think our relationship was only ever based on physical attraction.'

'Definitely could have done without hearing that.'

Natalie sat back and took a deep breath. 'You were never like that.'

'What, beautiful?'

Natalie laughed, properly laughed this time. I loved hearing it so much, I smiled involuntarily. 'No, Cowley—controlling, manipulative. You were always . . . cool.'

This time, I laughed. 'That's the first time anyone has ever described me as cool.'

'You were, though,' she said. 'You made me laugh. Oh God, how you made me laugh. Jez never did. He was always so bloody serious all the time. Everything was about the animals, or the poor people, or the poor animals. I mean, it's great to believe in stuff, but have a break every now and then.'

She looked at me. Her face was pale and her eyes puffy. 'You're quiet,' she said.

'I suppose I just don't know what to say. I mean, I came all the way here just to make sure you were OK, and now I think you will be.'

'Really?'

I nodded. 'Of course you will. You're strong and clever and funny and I know for a fact you'll never let another boy boss you around like that again.'

Natalie smiled kind of sadly and squeezed my arm. 'I miss you, Cowley.'

Now I really didn't know what to say.

She squeezed me again, this time harder. 'Did you hear me?'

I looked out at the dark field and then back at her. 'Yes,' I said.

Without warning, Natalie leaned across and tried to kiss me. I jumped to my feet.

« Older posts

Wait, what the hell are you doing? Hank cried.

This is a highly irregular strategy, said Norman.

Natalie stared at me, open-mouthed. I didn't know what to do. I suddenly became very aware of my hands. What did I normally do with them? I stuffed them in my pockets.

'I-I'm so sorry, Joe,' she said.

'Um, that's . . . OK?'

Natalie stood up. 'No, I really am. Just because I split up with Jez doesn't give me the right to kiss you. You have a girlfriend.'

'Honestly, it's fine.'

'I'm just sad, that's all,' she said. 'I didn't mean anything by it.'

I didn't know how I felt about that. My brain was like a washing machine full of Catherine wheels.

She pulled me in close for a hug. Oh God, she still smelled like Natalie. That sounds weird, but bear with me. You know when a person's smell stays with you, somewhere in the back of your mind, and you catch a whiff of it one day and loads of memories about that person come flooding back all at once? Well, that happened.

'You're a good guy, Cowley,' she said. 'Thank you so much for coming back.' She let go of me and tried to rub off the wet tears from my shirt. 'But that weirdness won't happen again. Promise.'

I'm sitting on the train to Leeds, watching the early morning sun rise over the fields. I'm glad it won't happen again.

I really am.

Tuesday 17th March

When I got to the TV 'studio' (someone's garage) in Leeds, I found things hadn't really improved. No one was really talking to each other. Mo told me that Harry had spent the whole journey sitting up front with her.

I can't wait until this tour is over. Kristoff will be a distant memory and we won't be living on top of each other in a crummy van.

After the interview, we got back in and headed for Glasgow. That was when I saw the email.

FROM: Natalie Tuft
TO: Joe Cowley
Subject: Last night
Hi Cowley,

Again, I'm really sorry about what happened. I

hope things are still cool between us.

To make it up to you, I want to help out the Sound Experience (I refuse to call them Xperience).

My mum's friend is a lawyer. Send me the contracts and I'll see if she can look them over.

Love,

Nat x

Luckily, I still had our copies in my bag, so I took photos of them on the iPad and sent them over to Natalie. I'm not sure how I feel about all this. I mean, if this lawyer finds some way of getting us out of the contract, it will be over, won't it?

Then again, there must be another record label who'll have us. Or maybe we don't need one.

When we arrived in Glasgow, I found Mila and Kristoff standing outside the stage door. Kristoff was smoking a self-rolled cigarette and seemed to be in the middle of some kind of ramble about art, or architecture, or how it's possible to have your head so firmly up your own jacksy without suffocating on your own crap.

Mila hugged me and asked if my family was OK.

'Everyone's fine,' I mumbled, guilt twisting my guts. 'Sorry I couldn't be there last night.'

'That's OK,' she said. 'I needed an early night, anyway.'

Hold on a sec, said Hank. *Does she mean early night as in early night, or early night as in EARLY NIGHT?*

'Hey, man,' said Kristoff. 'You stoked about heading to Europe?'

'Yeah,' I said. 'Stoked-on-Trent.'

'I was just telling Mila how psyched I am to play Amsterdam,' he droned. 'I can't wait to be up there, playing those chords that open the concert in front of my people. It's going be a spiritual moment, man.'

'I'm just looking forward to eating a big *stroopwafel* the size of a manhole cover,' said Mila. 'That's the main thing I've missed since moving to England.'

'Yeah, they're rad,' said Kristoff. 'My grandma used to make them all the time. If I have one in Amsterdam, it might be a little emotional for me, because she passed a couple of years ago. Could you come with me, Mila? Make sure I'm OK?'

'You'll have to excuse me,' I said. 'I have the sudden urge to vomit non-stop for seven years.'

Anyway, Glasgow went very much the same as every other night—the boys performed, Greeny got mobbed afterwards, Harry and Ad were ignored, and then we went back to the van. There was going to be no chance of meeting Mila because everyone was travelling overnight.

Marcy, Jackson, Mila, and the backing band were fly-

« Older posts

ing straight to Amsterdam from Glasgow airport. Not us, though. We had to drive to Newcastle with the stage crew and get a ferry.

Now, you've seen Amsterdam on a map, right? It looks proper close to Newcastle. So how long do you think it would take to get there by boat? Three hours? Four?

FIFTEEN HOURS. FIF-COCKING-TEEN.

Apparently, we can't fly over because we only have enough budget to use one vehicle. Yes, we have to drive around Europe in that heap of crap. And what is Mo going to be like driving over there? She'll cause World War Three!

Away from the claustrophobia of the van, everyone has taken the opportunity to split up. Greeny is lying asleep across a row of chairs, Harry is in a corner, reading a book about Napoleon, Dad and Mo are in the bar getting embarrassingly drunk, and I am by the window, watching Ad and Sebastian recreate the king of the world scene from Titanic at the railings.

Ugh, I can't believe this is happening. I bet Kristoff has weaselled his way next to Mila on the plane and is probably whispering in her ear about how great shite-waffles are and how he'll basically wee himself with excitement when he plays the opening chords at the gig.

I hope he chokes on his complimentary peanuts.

Wednesday 18th March

We pulled into Amsterdam harbour after the crossing from hell. About halfway there, the sea started getting rough and I immediately felt dead peaky. I tried to stand by the window and focus on the horizon but that didn't work.

Dad and Mo emerged from the bar. Mo was holding a coffee, probably because she needed to sober up.

'Not got your sea legs, pal?' she said to me. 'They don't call this ship the *Vomit Comet* for nothing.'

I tried to ignore her and screwed my eyes shut to blank out the swell of the ship.

'Your da and me have got a bet on,' she said. 'He's got twenty quid you won't puke, and I've got twenty you will. Don't let me down.'

As she said the word 'down', she slapped my back and an immense eruption of spew geysered out of my mouth and into the window. I would never make it as a pirate.

Mo cackled and tickled Dad. 'Come on then, pay up, you big rapping bugger.'

Even when we were back in the van, I still felt like I was on the boat. I sipped a bottle of water and tried to convince myself that I wasn't going to yak again. Not an easy task when your dad is right in front of you, changing his pants.

'Right, lads,' said Mo as we pulled out of the car park into the afternoon winter sun. 'Things you should know about Amsterdam—there are no railings by the canals. They assume you're clever enough to avoid falling in, so for Christ's sake keep an eye on Ad at all times.'

Ad nodded as if she had a point.

'Second thing—you're going to see women standing in windows. You don't need to know why they're there, just stay away. Third—if you're going to go to a coffee shop, avoid the brownies. Trust me on that. I had one of those last time I was here and I woke up three hours later in a skip. Other than that, it's a cracking wee town.'

She was right. The city centre is proper beautiful—all pretty canals and people sitting outside cafes. Nothing like Tammerstone. The only thing you'll find by our canals are dog crap and muggers. None of the others were really in the mood to explore, but Mila was helping out with Marcy promo all day and I had to do something to distract myself.

'So what shall we do?' I said, flipping through a guide book. 'Visit the Anne Frank house? Walk around the Vondelpark? Say hi to a window lady?'

'I've got a better idea, old son,' said Harry. 'According to

Verity's Instagram, they're in Amsterdam, too, staying in a Eurotraveller Hostel. We should go and meet them.'

I exchanged a quick look with Greeny. 'Are you sure that's a good—'

'Yes. Now come on,' said Harry.

We found the hostel in a dingy back street about ten minutes' walk from the centre. It looked kind of rough, but at least it wasn't a bloody camper van. Harry tried calling Verity and Ad tried calling Jasmeen, but they had no luck.

'So what do we do now?' I said. I was eager to do something else—all this standing around wasn't doing enough to distract me from the idea of Mila spending all day Dutching it up with Kristoff.

'We wait,' said Harry.

Luckily, we didn't have to wait long. I heard voices approaching around the corner which sounded unmistakably like Verity and Jasmeen. And two other voices that sounded unmistakably Australian.

When they actually emerged, my stomach twisted. They were all over each other. Jasmeen was even having a piggy back. Harry and Ad turned around.

'Oh,' said Verity. 'Harry. What are you doing here?'

She let go of Aussie #1's hand while Jasmeen jumped off Aussie #2's back.

'So these are your *friends,* are they?' said Harry.

'Look, mate, maybe you should relax,' said Aussie #1.

Harry glared at him as if his idea of relaxing was ripping off his head and punting it into the canal. 'Are you going to tell me what's going on?'

Verity sighed. 'I'm sorry, Harry. It's just not working long-distance. I should have told you sooner, but at least this way, you get to hear it face-to-face.'

Harry looked like he was about to crumple into a ball.

'Yeah,' said Jasmeen, staring at the floor. 'It's not working for me either.'

There was silence. It was like a stand-off in one of those old cowboy movies. I glanced at Harry. His eyes were full of tears. Oh no. This was weird. Too weird. In all the years I have known Harry, I have never seen him cry. Not even when we were five and I used to bawl at stuff like not being able to poke the straw into my Ribena carton.

I put my hand on his shoulder but he shrugged it off.

'So that's it, then?' he said. 'It's over?'

Verity nodded sadly. 'I hope we can still be friends.'

Harry laughed. 'Friends?' he said. 'Why the bloody hell would I be friends with someone who betrayed me?'

'We're sorry,' said Jasmeen. 'We didn't plan for this to happen.'

'Could have fooled me,' Aussie #2 muttered, causing Aussie #1 to splutter with laughter.

Harry roared and ran at Aussie #1. I tried to stop him, but he was away. I don't know why he didn't factor in the size difference. Aussie #1 was over six feet tall and built like the *HMS Belfast*. When Harry pummelled his chest with punches, he just lifted him above his head like he was nothing.

'Unhand me, you poltroon!' Harry yelled.

'I'll let you go when you chill out,' said Aussie #1.

'He'll chill,' I said, noticing a couple of police officers watching from over the road. 'Put him down.'

He did as I asked and Harry stormed away in the opposite direction, screaming obscenities.

Ad went up to Jasmeen. 'So . . . does this mean we're over, too?'

Jasmeen rolled her eyes. 'Yes, Ad.'

'Ah right,' he said, and walked off.

We found Harry pacing up and down by the canal. People were giving him a wide berth, probably thinking he was some kind of raving tramp boy.

« Older posts

'Come on, mate,' I said. 'Sit down for a bit, yeah?'

'Sit down?' he fumed. 'I've been sitting down long enough. It's time to stand up.'

'Joe, has Harry gone mental?' said Ad, his whisper about as quiet as your average military jet.

'This is all BOLLOCKS!' Harry yelled. 'It has been since the beginning. This bloody industry has taken my band away from me and now my girlfriend is history. Well, I have had enough!'

'Please, Harry,' said Greeny. 'You're going to get us all arrested.'

Harry stopped pacing and walked right at Greeny, getting in his face. 'Don't talk to me, you bloody traitor.'

'Traitor?' I said. 'Come on, Harry, that's enough.'

'Oh, you don't know do you, old bean?' said Harry. 'Old Greeny is leaving us.'

'What?' me and Ad said in unison.

Harry nodded. 'Going solo, aren't you? You've been chatting about it with Jackson. I heard you on the phone last night.'

I thought back to Marcy's warning. Looks like she was dead on.

'Is that right, Greeny?' said Ad.

Greeny's eyes went all watery and his chin wobbled. 'He was telling me I'd be able to bring Scott on tour,' he said. 'Plus, he kept going on about how you lot hate it and I'd be doing you a favour.'

I couldn't believe what I was hearing. We'd only been in Amsterdam for five minutes and it already felt like our entire world was imploding.

'Doing us a favour?' said Harry. 'You destroying everything I've ever worked for so you can go and mime awful songs and go home to your bloody boyfriend every night? I should kick you in the BALLS!'

I had never seen him this angry. It was freaking me out.

'I didn't agree to it, though,' said Greeny.

'But you didn't turn it down, did you?' said Harry, his eyes narrowed.

Greeny said nothing.

'Unbelievable,' said Harry. 'It really is. You know, I was against being friends with you from the beginning and now I'm beginning to see my first instinct was correct.'

Something snapped in Greeny, then. I could see it. He pushed Harry so hard, he smacked into the side of a bike rack.

'Shove your band up your arse, Harry,' he yelled. 'I'm going to find Jackson and tell him I'll sign.'

'Good,' Harry screamed. 'Because we don't NEED you!'

Harry stormed off one way, Greeny the other, leaving me and Ad standing there awkwardly.

'So,' said Ad. 'Do you want to go and look at Anne Frank-enstein's house?'

« Older posts

'Ad, that's . . . that's not . . . I'm . . . yes, OK, we'll go to Anne Frankenstein's house.'

I know it might seem weird doing touristy stuff after my friendship group basically just blew up, but I guess I was hoping that Harry and Greeny would cool down later and make up. There was no way we would end up like FTW.

Anyway, after a miserable time walking around the Anne Frank house and trying to explain to Ad that the only monsters involved in the story were the Nazis and not a massive bloke made of corpses, we went for a coffee. I hadn't slept properly in about twenty-four hours and was beginning to flag. When I had sat down with a drink and made sure Ad hadn't bought a brownie, I logged onto the cafe's Wi-Fi and checked my emails. There was one from Natalie.

FROM: Natalie Tuft
TO: Joe Cowley

Subject: The verdict is in . . .

COWLEY!
The contracts you signed are a load of C . . .

Thursday 19th March

I read the email. Then I read it again. And again. My head was spinning and I don't think it was from passive smoking.

'What's up, mate?' said Ad. 'You're not watching that video of the three girls and a sick bag are you?'

I shushed him and read again.

COWLEY!
The contracts you signed are a load of CRAP!!! My mum's friend said she'd never seen anything like it.

You have literally NO say in anything. He could ship you to Siberia and have you jigging for Eskimos and there would be nothing you could do about it.

You were supposed to have received advance payments. This bit is buried right in the middle of the small print, but it is in there. You were due £1500 and the others were due £3000 each. Did you receive that? If not, where is the money?

« Older posts

If you haven't been paid, she reckons this could be clear proof of money embezzlement, which means you've got him. YOU'VE GOT HIM!

Freedom can be yours, Cowley, if you want it.

Love,
Nat x

I gulped. It was all so much to take in.

'What's up, Joe?' said Ad.

I shook my head quickly and put my phone on standby. 'Nothing. Just reading an interesting article.'

I could have just told him, but something stopped me. What would happen if I got us out of our contracts? I wouldn't have a job, I wouldn't have a nice flat in London, I wouldn't even have a bedroom. I'd have to go back home and bed down on the sofa bed next to two angry gnomes.

Maybe if I just hung on a little longer, I'd be able to change things. I decided to have a word with Jackson and ask him about the money. Maybe it was just a mistake and he would pay up. Maybe he'd be so ashamed, we'd get a nice bus and decent hotel rooms to stay in. Maybe he'd forget about trying to get Greeny to go solo and let us do our own thing.

Let's cut the crap, said Hank. Y*ou've caught wiggy boy with his hand in the cash register and now you have some-thing to blackmail him with.*

I called Jackson but he didn't answer. I tried again.

'What?'

'Um, hello, Jackson. I need to speak to you about our contracts.'

The line went quiet. Ad looked even more confused than he normally does.

'Well, it'll have to wait—we have a full day of promo with Marcy and a PA in a nightclub tonight.'

'Fine,' I said. 'Can we meet tomorrow morning?'

He grumbled swear words under his breath. 'All right. I'm at the Marriott—room 237. Don't come too early.'

This morning at eight, I was at his door. I didn't get much sleep anyway. Partly because Dad kept trying to spoon me and partly because of the sheer horrible tension. Harry wouldn't speak to anyone and Greeny didn't even come back at all. He texted me to say he was staying in a cheap hotel.

Jackson answered the door in a bathrobe. Everything about him was messy except his hair, which was exactly the same as it always is.

'I said not too early, Joe,' he snapped.

'Sorry,' I said. 'I'm an early riser.'

He shook his head and gestured for me to follow him into the room. I felt sick. This was the nicest hotel room I'd seen in my life. Even better than the one I stayed in with Mila when I had Afghan-food-related bum explosions.

Jackson slumped in a chair by the window. 'So what's up?'

I took a deep breath. Part of me wanted to run away and hide in the van, but I knew I couldn't. I would have felt like I was letting Natalie down.

'Where's our money?' I blurted out.

I had this whole speech planned about how our legal counsel had examined the documents, but all I could get out were those three words. To be fair, they did kind of cut to the point.

Jackson took a sip of coffee and looked at me as if I'd asked him where he kept his alien egg incubator.

'What are you on about?' he said.

'The money,' I said again. 'We were supposed to have been paid.'

My legs were shaking but the more I tried to disguise it, the worse they became. I was like Shaggy from *Scooby Doo.*

Jackson chuckled without smiling. 'And what makes you think that?'

'Our contracts,' I said. 'We got a lawyer to look through them.'

Jackson shot out of his chair and into my face. 'Are you some sort of clever dick?'

Well, you're half right, said Hank.

'Do you know who you're messing with?' he went on.

I gulped and tried to remember what I went there to say.

'I want you to stop interfering with the SOUND EXPERIENCE and leave Greeny alone.'

Jackson got closer to me. His breath was horrible.

'Or what?'

'Or I'll report you for stealing our money.'

He laughed and gripped my shoulder. 'You'd do that, would you?'

I couldn't look into his eyes. It was like going face-to-face with a shark.

'Yes,' I said.

He squeezed harder. 'If you do that, if you really think that is a good idea—I will ruin you. I will see to it that you

and your boys never work in this industry again. I've got contacts who owe me favours all over the world at record labels, papers, everything, and they will bury you without a trace.'

My insides burned with rage. I imagined myself karate-kicking him right in the face and rifling through his wallet for the money he took from us. I couldn't do anything, though.

'Now get out before I really lose my temper,' he said.

I did as I was told.

What the hell was all that about? Hank yelled when I got outside. *Get back in there and kick his ass!*

No, Joe, said Norman. *Violence solves nothing.*

Yeah, but it makes you feel better, said Hank, *whacking Norman on the head with a clipboard.*

When I turned up at Mila's hotel room, she asked me what was wrong.

'What's wrong?' I said. 'What's cocking wrong? Jackson is screwing us!'

'What do you mean?' she said.

I explained to her everything I had found out, but she

didn't seem that bothered.

'I'm sure there has been some mistake,' she said. 'Jackson isn't corrupt—I mean, look at the success he's had.'

'Yeah, because he intimidates people into doing what he says,' I said.

Mila linked her hands behind my neck. 'That's just how the music industry is.'

'Bull crap!' I yelled, yanking myself free. 'This hasn't been right since day one and every time I've tried to talk about it with you, you've fobbed me off.'

'Fobbed you off?' she said, frowning.

'You didn't listen!' I said, remembering that some English phrases make no sense. 'You were too busy going on about how brilliant Kristoff is.'

Mila groaned. 'Oh God, Joe, enough. Kristoff is just my friend.'

'Is he, though?' I said. 'The fact is, you wish he was your boyfriend, not me. I bet when you found out you were staying in hotels together, you were cocking ECSTATIC!'

I'm not sure how this had stopped being about Jackson and started being about Kristoff, but it had, and I wasn't about to apologize.

Mila gasped and slapped me across the face. 'Get out,' she growled. 'I hate you!'

I did as I was told and scarpered into the corridor, the door slamming behind me. I told myself that the tears in

« Older posts

my eyes were caused by the sting of the slap and not Mila saying she hates me.

I didn't want to go back to the van, so I just walked the streets. It was such a pretty day it seemed perverse to be so miserable. I still was, though.

I spent the next four hours wandering around Amsterdam, going through everything in my head—no wonder Jackson can afford a condo in the Bahamas when he robs people left, right, and cocking centre and gets away with it. My mind zoomed back to my few days with Niles.

'If I had all the money I was entitled to, I could buy this entire hotel,' he said.

At the time I didn't think anything of it, but now it made sense. I carried on walking, not knowing where I was heading, cursing Jackson and Mila.

I understand your anger, Joe, Norman said when my brain cleared enough to allow the control room to appear. *But is any of this Mila's fault?*

Well, no, but she hasn't helped.

But is it her fault?

The streets were beginning to get more crowded with people on their lunch breaks when I realized I had been too hard on Mila. I was just so angry about Jackson that I took it out on her. I had to make it up to her.

First, I bought her a bunch of flowers. I remember Dad always used to buy Mum lilies after they'd had a row. I mean, yeah, they ended up getting a divorce, but that's beside the point.

I was about to head back to the hotel when I remembered something. It would elevate my gesture from a standard flowers apology to something a bit more personal.

I arrived at the hotel with flowers in one hand and a massive *stroopwafel* in the other. The sign said they were the best *stroopwafels* in Amsterdam.

I found Mila's room and knocked on the door with the flowers under my arm. We'd never had a big argument before so I was hoping she'd forgive me.

I could hear footsteps approaching the door. And a voice.

'Wow, the room service here is fast.'

The door opened and my heart sank. Actually, no, 'my heart sank' doesn't cover it. My heart smashed into an iceberg, broke in half and plunged to the floor of the Atlantic.

'Oh, Joe,' said Kristoff, standing in the doorway wearing a dressing gown. 'Man, this is awkward.'

Maybe there's an innocent explanation for this, said Norman.

What, someone stole all his freakin' clothes and she's giving him a safe haven while the police dust his room for prints? said Hank. *Do you hear yourself when you talk?*

« Older posts

Then, Mila appeared behind him, wearing what looked like one of Kristoff's shirts.

'Joe,' she said.

But I was away.

I heard her voice echoing down the corridor behind me, saying she was sorry, and it only happened because she was sad, but I didn't want to hear it. I dumped the flowers in a bin in the lobby and Frisbee'd the gloopwaffle at a wall.

There was this horrible burning feeling in my brain and my guts were churning. I've never felt pain like it. All of a sudden I got it—what I put Natalie through when I kissed Lisa. I thought I understood before, but I really didn't. That feeling of betrayal and knowing you're not good enough stings like hell. Maybe this was that karma thing people are always going on about.

Before I knew where I was, I was back at the van. Harry

and Greeny were having a stand-up row by their bunks but when I walked in all the attention turned to me.

'Oh, here he is!' Harry yelled. 'The reason we're in this mess.'

'What are you on about?' I mumbled.

'Jackson called us, Joe,' said Ad, sitting in the corner with Sebastian on his lap. 'He said if we're so unhappy about being on this tour we should thank you cos it was your idea.'

Ah crap, said Hank.

I could have tried to deny it, but what would have been the point? 'OK,' I said. 'It's true. I just wanted to get you some exposure.'

Greeny grabbed me by the shoulders. 'Exposure? I nearly had a nervous breakdown!'

'Of all the bloody stupid things you've done, this ranks at number bloody one,' Harry said. 'Well, I hope you're proud because you've ruined everything. There is no more SOUND EXPERIENCE.'

'Why did you really do it, Joe?' said Ad. 'Cos even I knew that rubbish music we were making didn't need no exposure.'

I took some shaky breaths. 'I know it's stupid,' I said. 'But I only did it because I didn't want Mila to go on tour with that Kristoff cos I thought she was going to cheat on me with him and nowshehasandlaaaaarrggh.'

« Older posts

Yeah, I started sobbing. It was really embarrassing. And the more I tried to stop myself, the worse it became.

Greeny loosened his grip on my shoulders and instead started awkwardly rubbing my back. Harry and Ad joined in.

All the noise must have alerted Dad and Mo because they came in to join the pity party.

Great, Snoop Dad and Rowdy Roddy Piper are here, said Hank. *That's all we freakin' need.*

'Hey, son,' said Dad. 'What's going down?'

Mo stepped in front of him and said, 'Let me handle this, Keith.' Then she grabbed me and yelled, 'Why the bloody hell are you crying?'

I tried to answer but I couldn't get the words out.

'Is it that girl?' she said.

I nodded.

'Has she gone off with that piano player?'

I nodded again.

I heard Harry say, 'Oh bloody hell,' behind me.

'Did you slap the nut on him?' said Mo.

I shook my head.

'You disappoint me, wee man,' she said. 'Now, come on. Pull yourself together.'

I tried to slow my breathing down but it just made it worse and I ended up making a noise like a distressed cow on helium.

Mo gripped me around the back of my head with one hand

and screamed, 'I SAID, PULL YOURSELF TOGETHER, SOLDIER.'

I was so startled, I actually stopped crying.

Mo pressed her forehead against mine, sending gusts of smoky breath straight up my nose.

'Real men don't cry, do you understand?' she yelled. 'Real men keep their emotions inside until they have to drown them in booze or take up bare knuckle boxing.'

Actually, I'm not sure that's right, said Norman.

'When I was taking shelter in a Kuchi tent in the middle of the Afghan mountains, with an empty gun and a carful of Taliban outside baying for my blood, did I start crying?' she said, pressing her head into mine so hard by this point, we were almost becoming conjoined twins. 'No, I bloody didn't. I strolled out, pointed at the biggest bugger there and challenged him to wrestle, right there in the dirt. If I won, they'd let me go. If he won, I'd be their prisoner.'

'So what happened?' I asked.

'Still here, aren't I?' said Mo.

I'm sure I heard Harry whisper something about Mo

« Older posts

being the coolest person alive.

'So do you see what I'm trying to say to you, pal?' she went on.

'Y-you want me to wrestle Kristoff?'

'No, you soft git,' she said. 'I'm saying you need to be the big man. Get out there and make that silly girl see what a huge mistake she's made.'

'But that's not all,' I said, pulling away before she crushed my skull in. 'We have another problem as well.'

'We?' said Harry.

I nodded. 'I've had the contracts checked and Jackson has been screwing us over this whole time.'

'You what?' said Ad.

'The contracts have been checked and they say you are entitled to three grand each. Jackson must have pocketed the lot.'

For a few seconds, the only sound that could be heard was Mo breathing like a bull with anger management issues.

'You have got to be bloody kidding me,' said Harry. 'Still want to sign a solo deal with him, Greeny?'

'No I don't,' he said. 'If he's willing to screw us like that, he'll have no problem breaking his promises to me. To be honest, I was never going to do it, anyway. I was just letting you believe I was because you were acting like such a knob.'

'I can't believe it,' said Dad. 'Jackson seemed like such a cool dude.'

Mo leaned closer to us and spoke quietly. 'Give me five minutes alone in a room with him and I'll get your money.'

Harry nodded. 'As entertaining as that would be, I don't think it is the best course of action. I suggest we don't bother turning up for the gig tonight and tell him to shove it.'

'I don't know,' I said. 'He told me if we do anything like that, he'll make sure we never work in the music industry again.'

There was silence as we all looked at each other. After a while, Harry spoke up.

'Do we even want to work in this bloody industry?'

I thought about Jackson and Kristoff and how I hate them both more than I have ever hated anyone. Then I thought about people like Niles and Marcy. Did I want it to get to the stage where all my friends hate each other?

'I don't think I do, actually,' I said. 'How about you guys?'

Greeny shook his head. Then Ad did.

Harry smiled. It was the first time I'd seen him do that in ages.

'Very good, old beans,' he said. 'But while you were deliberating, I had a rethink.'

Me and Ad grinned at each other.

'Have you come up with a strategy?' I said.

Harry pulled a pipe I thought was long gone out of his

« Older posts

pocket and clamped it between his teeth. 'Let's just say I'm formulating some ideas.'

2.15 a.m.

We arrived at the venue nice and early. There had been loads of hype in the Dutch press about the gig and it sold out within five minutes. It was even being broadcast on live TV for everyone who couldn't get tickets. In other words, it was a big deal.

When Jackson arrived and saw us ready to go on, he smirked at me and said, 'Glad to see you've decided not to do anything rash. I'd hate for four such promising careers to hit the skids so soon.'

I ignored him and tried to focus on the task at hand. I was worried about running into Mila and turning into a blubbering mess again, but luckily she had stayed away.

When the production manager gave XPERIENCE the go-ahead to walk on stage, the four of us exchanged a quick look. It was nothing so obvious that Jackson would notice, but it was enough to signify that Harry's plan was ready to be put into action.

Once they were gone, I left Jackson by the monitors and headed out to the arena to watch from the photographer's run at the front of the stage.

'Good evening, Amsterdam,' said Harry into a live mic. 'We are the *SOUND EXPERIENCE*.'

I could almost hear Jackson's head popping from back-stage. But that was nothing compared to what they had in store.

« Older posts

Sirens filled the auditorium, followed by a robotic voice booming, 'KAMIKAZE ATTACK.' Hologram planes flew out from the stage as green lights whizzed through the air.

If they were going out for good, they might as well do it on their own terms. For the first time ever, I was actually enjoying their music, dancing and pumping my fists.

Just before show time, Harry and Ad sneaked onto the stage and connected all their equipment to the PA, so it could actually be heard. While they were doing that, Greeny hacked into Marcy Slick's effects unit and loaded the *SOUND EXPERIENCE*'s projections.

Of course, all of this could have been overridden by the techs in the sound booth, which is why it was lucky we had an insane Glaswegian van driver to go in there and persuade them that they probably shouldn't. When I glanced back that way and saw the terrified looks on their faces, I felt satisfied that the *SOUND EXPERIENCE* would get to play their whole set.

And what a set it was. I mean, yeah, half the crowd loved it and the half the crowd looked like they were witnessing some kind of mine disaster, but that's what makes the *SOUND EXPERIENCE* great. Strip them of their weirdness and they become boring. I got out my phone and took a photo of them onstage—Harry working the drum machine, his pipe jutting out of his mouth, Ad with his glasses glinting in the stage lights, and Greeny doing what he truly loves to do:

create awesome effects.

After 'Dive, Dive, Dive', Harry grabbed the mic again and said, 'That was our last song. We have been the *SOUND EXPERIENCE* and all that is left for us to say is that Jackson McHugh of PGS Records is a money embezzler who can cram his contracts straight up his stupid old arse. Goedenacht!'

As they left the stage, I ran straight around the back to meet them. Before I could get there, Marcy stopped me.

'If you're going to go out, you should do it in style,' she said, shaking my hand. 'All the best in whatever you decide to do. You're too nice a guy for this industry.'

I said thanks and got on my way to join the others. I had a feeling Jackson was going to be after me.

'What the hell was that all about?' he screamed at us as we walked away.

« Older posts

We just carried on and ignored him.

'You will never work again!' he yelled as we boarded the van. 'Do you hear me? NEVER!'

Dad appeared from the other side of the van. 'Wait a sec, dawg. I think y'all need to chillax.'

Jackson turned his pinprick shark eyes on Dad. 'Listen, you pathetic old man, I gave you this job so you could control your idiot son. What have you been doing?'

'All right, pal?' Mo came up behind him.

'Push off, you stupid pleb,' Jackson spat.

We crowded around the window and watched as Mo smiled and said, 'The lads have a message for you.'

'Oh yeah?' said Jackson. 'What is it?'

Mo's smile flipped to a scowl before she went to 'slap the nut' on Jackson, but stopped a millimetre short then snatched the wig right off his head.

'Give that back!' Jackson screamed.

Mo grabbed Dad around the waist and pushed him inside the van, then put the wig on her head, got in behind him and gunned it out of the car park.

We must have spent the first ten minutes of the journey cheering and dancing around the van. We couldn't believe we had pulled it off. We had reclaimed the *SOUND EXPERI-ENCE* and escaped the evil clutches of Baldy McHugh. It couldn't get any better.

Or so I thought.

'Actually, old boy,' said Harry. 'We did arrange a special surprise for you.' He checked his watch. 'And it is just about to start.'

He switched on the tiny crappy TV in the van and flicked through the channels until he found the start of the Marcy Slick concert. Kristoff was on-screen, a big, smug grin on his face. He must have thought this was the greatest day of his life—he steals my girlfriend and gets to play his stupid chords in front of his people and blah, blah, blah.

Kristoff pumped the keys. But the chords didn't come out. Not the real ones anyway. What came out instead was the loudest fart sound I've ever heard in my life.

Harry, Ad, and Greeny started laughing their arses off as Kristoff frantically changed the setting on his keyboard and tried again, only for more squelchy farts to come out.

Harry patted my shoulder. 'While we were setting up our gear, we decided to do a little bit of DIY on lover boy's keyboard. We thought you'd approve.'

'This is the nicest thing you guys have ever done for me,' I said.

The others smiled and we all piled in for a four-way man hug while the explosive farts continued to rip out of the TV.

'So,' said Greeny to Harry after we broke up, 'are we OK now?'

Harry held out his hand. 'Course we are, old bean.'

'Hey,' said Ad as the concert cut to an emergency commercial break, 'I know a song Kristoff could play on that keyboard—"My Fart Will Go On".'

We all laughed.

'Or "Trump and Grind",' said Greeny.

'How about "Shite Fever"?' I said.

'Boys, boys, boys,' said Harry. 'I think we know that there is only one winner in this instance, and that is "Poohemian Crapsody".'

And we carried on like that for hours. It was just like the old days.

I guess that even though I've lost my girlfriend, my career, and my entire purpose in life, at least I'll always have my friends. My weird, pretend-pipe-smoking, nude-sleepwalking, half-genius, half-moron friends.

Saturday 21st March

Well, I'm home.

It took us nearly two whole days of driving to get back from Amsterdam, which was kind of horrible, but at least it gave the four of us time to just be mates again. To talk about stuff that was nothing to do with interviews or recording sessions. For us to play round after disgusting round of Would You Rather?

It also gave us time to send out emails to President Ampleforth, as well as all the big music blogs, telling them exactly what kind of scam Jackson McHugh has been running. Yeah, he might be able to weasel his way out of it, but the point is that we figured him out. Plus, Mo has his wig, so you know, there's that.

I was expecting everyone to be miserable, but we weren't at all. I think the whole thing made us realize that *SOUND EXPERIENCE* are better off putting out their music themselves. No one will try and smooth off their weird edges or take advantage of them.

When we stopped for a toilet break, I sent this:

Natalie,

You'll be pleased to know we're out of our contract. Thanks so much—we couldn't have done it without you.

« Older posts

The other thing is, Mila and I are over. I found her cheating on me with some arse from Marcy Slick's backing band. It made me want to tell you I'm sorry again. I felt everything you felt that night in Trafalgar Square and it was horrible. The thought that I made you feel like that is the worst.

Anyway, thanks for staying in touch through all this. At times, you've been the only sane person in my life and I really needed that.

Love,
Cowley

She messaged me back pretty much straight away.

Cowley,

I'm glad it's all worked out. And thanks—it means a lot.

Jez came to see me yesterday. He says he made a mistake and wants to get back together. He says he's changed and will stop telling me what to do. Conflicted, to say the least.

Nat x

Whatever she decides, I hope it works out for her. She deserves that.

When Mo dropped us off at the flat, I asked her if she was going to be OK, what with being sacked and everything.

'I'll be fine, wee man,' she said, Jackson's wig perched on her head like roadkill. 'There's always work for good drivers.'

'So what are you going to do, then?' said Ad. I trod on his foot to shut him up.

'Well, if it doesn't work out, you can always sell the wig,' said Harry.

'No way, pal,' she said. 'Back in the days of the old West, Native American warriors would claim the scalps of their fallen foes as proof of their victory. I see this as a continuation of that tradition.'

'Wow,' Harry whispered.

I noticed Dad was still in the passenger seat. 'Dad, are you coming, or what?'

He leaned over and smiled. 'No, son, I'm staying with Mo,' he said. 'Even though we have only known each other for a short time, we're mad tight, yo.'

Then Mo grabbed Dad and kissed him ferociously. I averted my eyes.

'Well isn't that sweet?' said Harry. 'Disgusting but sweet.'

« Older posts

'The heart wants what it wants, son,' said Dad after they broke off. 'Oh, Ad, buddy. Imma need that book back.'

Ad shrugged and threw *The Art of Love* to Dad.

Mo nodded at us. 'Goodbye, brothers, it has been an honour to serve with you.' Then she drove off and nearly ran over the postman.

It was weird being back in the flat and packing up all my stuff. I was sad in a way, because I was saying goodbye to my first taste of independence. And let's face it—I'm never going to have my own swanky flat in London again, am I? But in another way, I was glad to be leaving. Everything about it reminded me of Mila, of how naive I was. I just wanted to reach through the space–time continuum and give past me a firm slap.

Harry, Greeny, and Ad (accompanied by Sebastian) arranged to be interviewed by this underground music magazine that does exposés about shady music industry practices. They wanted me to go with them but I said no. I'd had enough of talking about the record industry.

I called Mum to see if she could come and pick me up. I had far too much stuff to go by train. She told me that she, Jim, and the twins were on holiday in Cornwall. She did mention it before, but with all the craziness, I forgot. There was no way I was going to stay in London for another three days, so I called Gav to see if he knew of anyone with a car. He said he'd ask around. I wasn't exactly relishing the idea of spending a two-hour car journey with one of Gav's associates, but beggars can't be choosers.

I had just about finished packing all my stuff when my phone rang. I guessed it must have been my driver. I was wrong.

'Joooeee! How's things, my man? It's Niles!'

'Oh, um, hi.'

'I'm out of the joint now and ready to fly,' he said. 'I've signed with a new record label and my debut solo album is going to drop next week, with a tour to follow.'

'Congratulations,' I said, wondering why he wanted to let me know, of all people.

'Anyways, I hear you're a free agent now,' he said.

In more ways than one, said Hank.

'Well . . . yes.'

'So I was going to offer you a job,' he said. 'You can be my assistant on tour.'

I didn't know what to say.

'Come on,' he said. 'We'll have a blast—you and me on the road, living it up!'

Do it, said Hank. *It'll be awesome—you can have the excess groupies!*

You are disgusting, said Norman. *Now, Joe, think about this carefully. Do you really want to throw yourself back into that world? You've seen how dangerous it can be.*

« Older posts

'Um, Niles?' I said. 'Did you say you've only just got out of jail?'

'Like I said, dude, fresh out of the clink.'

I thought for a couple of seconds. 'So how did you manage to record an album?'

Niles chuckled softly. 'All right, Joe, you got me. I'll come clean. I recorded that months ago. My management wanted me to be completely different from FTW so they suggested I get in a little bit of trouble—create a wild-child image.'

'Wait a minute,' I said. 'You got yourself arrested to promote your new album?'

Niles laughed again. 'When you put it like that, it sounds bad, but . . . yeah, that pretty much covers it.'

I couldn't believe what I was hearing.

'Don't you get sick of it?' I asked him. 'Getting exploited?'

Niles went quiet for a second, then said, 'Meh. What else am I going to do? Work in McDonald's?'

I wished him all the best with the tour, but there's no way I'm going. I mean, what will he do next to increase his notoriety? A flamethrower massacre?

While I was on the phone, I got a text from Gav.

Car will b there in a couple of hours. C u lata.

I sat down on the massive leather sofa and killed time by binge-watching **STAR TREK: TNG** series five.

I'm definitely going to miss having my own place. At the same time, I was kind of looking forward to being back home, where my mum will wash my pants for me and I'll get to see my little sisters grow up.

I got up and strolled around the flat one last time. The kitchen was bare except for Mrs Gleba's rules board (which by this point had willies doodled all over it) and a drawing stuck to the fridge. It was a copy of the one I drew of Mila at *BUZZFEST* last year. She made it for me as a house-warming present when we first moved in. It hurt to look at it, so my first instinct was to rip it up and throw it away. I couldn't, though. I felt like it had to stay here, like I could seal all the crap I'd been through for the last few months in this flat and that once I left, it would be trapped in there, like some kind of really depressing genie.

A car honked outside. I looked out of the window and saw it idling by the kerb. I took one last look at the flat and dragged my stuff out—a suitcase in each hand and a bag on each shoulder. It didn't look like this driver was coming to help, so I lugged it all down by myself.

Even though I'm glad to be leaving the music business, I still felt the cannonball of sadness sitting in my gut. I couldn't believe how much had changed—when I arrived in London, I had a new career and a girlfriend. Now, I'm leaving with no job, no prospects and no one to go home to. Greeny has Scott, Harry and Ad will be busy making music. What am I going to do?

I was about to drop my stuff in the boot when a

throat-clearing noise stopped me.

'Oh,' I said. 'Hi.'

My driver leaned against the car, her purple hair glinting in the sun and a wicked smile on her black lips.

'Where to, Cowley?' she said.

BEN DAVIS

Since he was a little boy, people told Ben Davis he would grow up to be an author. He didn't listen at the time, because he thought he was going to be an astronaut or play up front for Man United. When he reached his mid-twenties without a call from NASA/Fergie, he realized that maybe they had a point and started writing again. First, Ben wrote jokes for everything from radio shows to greeting cards. Then, he moved on to stories. He chose to write for young adults, largely because his sense of humour stopped maturing at the age of fifteen. Ben lives in Tamworth with his wife, son, and dog.

Find out more about Ben at the
Not So Private Blog of Ben Davis:
bendavisauthor.blogspot.co.uk

You can also visit his website:
bendavisauthor.com

Other cringe-filled books about Joe Cowley . . .

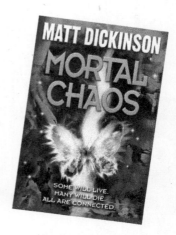

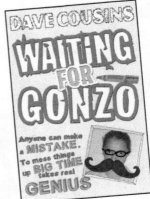

More fantastic
books
I reckon you'll like.